"Oh, for pity's sake!"

Kiel shook his head in disgust. "Do we really have to play this charade out to the bitter end? He left a note saying you were going away together!"

"What?" Shocked, Justine lurched upright. "Don't be so ridiculous! Why on earth would David and I go away together?"

"How the hell should I know? The idea of him wanting you as his mistress defies all comprehension!"

"His mistress? Don't be absurd! And don't be so bloody rude!"

"Rude? I'd like to exterminate you!" he ground out furiously. "You are the most selfish, amoral woman it's ever been by misfortune to come across!"

EMMA RICHMOND says she's amiable, undomesticated and an incurable romantic. And, she adds, she has a very forbearing husband, three daughters and a dog of uncertain breed. They live in Kent. A great variety of jobs filled her earlier working years, and more recently she'd been secretary to the chairman of a group of companies. Now she devotes her entire day to writing, although she hasn't yet dispelled her family's illusions that she's reverting to the role of housekeeper and cook! Emma finds writing obsessive, time-consuming—and totally necessary to her well-being.

Books by Emma Richmond

HARLEQUIN PRESENTS
1230–UNWILLING HEART
1317–HEART IN HIDING
1373–A TASTE OF HEAVEN
1421–LAW OF POSSESSION
1461–A FOOLISH DREAM
1516–UNFAIR ASSUMPTIONS
1582–A STRANGER'S TRUST

EMMA Richmond

DELIBERATE PROVOCATION

Harlequin Books

TORONTO • NEW YORK • LONDON
AMSTERDAM • PARIS • SYDNEY • HAMBURG
STOCKHOLM • ATHENS • TOKYO • MILAN
MADRID • WARSAW • BUDAPEST • AUCKLAND

ISBN 0-373-11624-1

DELIBERATE PROVOCATION

CHAPTER ONE

AN ENORMOUS yawn almost dislocated her jaw; her thick brown lashes lifted to reveal eyes of a startling lavender. Blinking once or twice to clear her vision, Justine stared blankly before her. Dust motes danced in the beams that slanted through the louvred blinds, ephemeral, fairy-like, and about as substantial as her thoughts. In her mind were pictures, images, fragmented, like old film clips that had a linking theme if only one could guess what it was. Fretful and resentful at her inability to recall recent events, she sighed. She had been so sure that when she woke again she would remember.

Transferring her gaze to the vase of daffodils that stood on the bedside locker, she stared at the card that was propped beside it as though even that unlikely object might hold the answer, although in all probability it was only a copy of the hospital rules, and rules and regulations were something she didn't care tuppence about. Not at this precise moment anyway. She'd been in a car crash, that she knew, not from remembering but because the doctor had told her so. She had a fractured wrist, cuts and bruises, and concussion, and the trite phrases trotted out to her by the medical staff, that it was quite normal not to remember the hours prior to an accident, that she had been lucky, that in a few days she would be out and about, only made her feel more resentful. Justine hated being out of control, not able to direct her life. She'd had enough of that as a child, always at the mercy of other people's whims, and she had sworn that never again would she allow herself to be put in that position. To survive in this world, you had to be strong, capable.

With an impatient little shake of her head, she brought her mind back to the matter in hand. What the devil had she been doing in her cousin David's car, for goodness' sake? Had she borrowed it? Yet why should she when she had a car of her own? Pushing irritably at the fall of long, straight brown hair that hung untidily across her shoulder, she stared disagreeably at the plaster cast that weighted her arm to the bed. How the hell was she to manage with her arm in plaster?

Hearing the door open, and thankful for the distraction, she turned her head, then groaned in dismay when she saw who it was. She supposed it had been too much to hope for that *he* wouldn't come back. She wasn't sure she had the energy for any more arguments. And there would be arguments, there always were with him, because the wretched man always, but always, managed to put her back up.

'You have remembered?' he demanded bluntly.

'No, I haven't,' she denied shortly as she stared into sea-green eyes that were as cold and deep as the fiords that had no doubt spawned him, 'and if you've come to finish your interrogation you're wasting your time. I have no more idea now than I did this morning why I was in David's car. Maybe I borrowed it!'

'Why would you borrow it?'

'I don't know, do I? If I did, I'd tell you, believe me!' And she would, even if only to get rid of him. He'd come marching in that morning looking like some ancient Viking god who'd just stepped off the prow of a longship, and to whom rape and pillage would be commonplace events. They'd had the same pointless question and answer session then as now, except that she'd drifted off to sleep in the middle of it which had no doubt infuriated him. Feeling crotchety and irritable, and somehow lost, she added peevishly, 'And I wish you'd stop looming over me, I find it very irritating!'

'You find everything irritating,' he retorted dismissively.

Knowing only too well the futility of denying it, she agreed sweetly, 'How true.'

Staring at her, his carved face a study in dislike, he commanded, 'Think!'

'I am thinking! I've done very little else since you stormed in here!'

'And?'

'And nothing! And your commanding me in that tone of voice, as though just your instruction is enough to make me remember, is practically guaranteed to make me do just the opposite!'

With a look of derision, he prowled across to the window and bent to peer through the slatted blinds. 'Whatever tone I used, you would be obstructive.'

Well, that was probably true, she thought tiredly; the man was a pain. Clever, complex, and utterly ruthless, and the only way to deal with him was to be as assertive as he was himself; squash any weaknesses that he could exploit. Closing her eyes, she made a superhuman effort to shut out his disturbing presence. Unfortunately, it did no such thing, only seemed to increase the tension that was almost thick enough to cut with a knife, and the sheer vitality of the man seemed to sap what little strength she had left.

'You think I am not entitled to interrogation?' he demanded wearily. 'Or Katia?' His rather grating voice, which made it sound as though words were unfamiliar to him, or left a nasty taste in his mouth, seemed to rasp along her nerve-endings, irritating her further. She couldn't imagine anything softening him, deflecting him from his chosen course. He'd have been a real asset to the police, she decided sourly. Half Norwegian, champion skier, designer and builder of boats, on the boards of several marine engineering companies, wealthy and domineering. An arrogant giant, and she disliked him intensely. As he did her. He'd told her once that she was aggressive and unfeminine. Aggressive, she would grant—even forthright, strong, because she'd always had to be—but unfeminine? Admittedly she liked to have her own way, and generally thought she always knew best, but unfeminine? Unfortunately, because his sister Katia was married to her cousin David, they were forced to meet occasionally, but that didn't mean she had to like him.

David didn't like him either, she mused ruminatively, as she glowered at his broad back, and small wonder. Kiel Lindstrom and David Naughton were about as unlike as any two men could be. Kiel arrogant and assured, David gentle, a dreamer.

'Look,' he began again, clearly in an effort to be reasonable when his expression only indicated his desire to shake her. 'You were found less than a mile from Gatwick——'

'I am very well aware where I was found,' she agreed bitingly, 'and going over and over it won't do you a bit of good. The doctor said I might never remember...'

'Oh, terrific. Today is Tuesday, and before next Monday I have to have found David. He's your cousin——'

'Stepcousin,' she corrected automatically.

'Stepcousin,' he agreed through clenched teeth, 'but apart from his mother you are his only relative, yes?'

'You know very well that I'm his only relative, and I don't for the life of me see what clarifying our relationship is going to achieve!'

'It will achieve nothing if you don't stop interrupting me!' Clearly holding his temper on a very fragile rein, he took a deep breath before resuming, 'So, you are the only one who might know where he is.' When she remained silent, he grated, 'So where might he go?'

'I don't know. I don't! I truly cannot remember. All I know is that I was found beside his car. Obviously there had been an accident,' she added slowly as her mind remained infuriatingly empty of any knowledge of David or why she should have been in his car. Struggling to grasp fragments of memory that hovered tantalisingly out of reach, she glared at him when he sighed. Deeply. 'Look, I've already had the police in wanting a statement, which I was unable to supply, so why you think I'll remember for you when I couldn't for them I can't imagine.'

'Can't you?' he asked derisively.

'No. All I know is that another car went out of control when its tyre burst, that it careered across the road, hit my offside wing and pushed me into the ditch. I do not remember it, have absolutely no recollection at all, so I am sorry, but I cannot help you. I would like to help you,' she added with a reasonableness that put his teeth on edge, 'but I can't.'

Making a sound of disgust in the back of his throat, he thumped his fist impotently against the wall. His shoulders hunched moodily, he irritably parted the blind and stared down into the hospital grounds. When Justine gave a gasp of distress as the bright sunlight stabbed painfully into her eyes, he grudgingly apologised before allowing the blind to fall back into place. 'All right, so where does he usually go?' he asked with monumental patience as he leaned his back against the wall. 'Places he's been before, a bolt-hole, anything. You must know something about him, for God's sake!'

'Well, I don't,' she denied moodily. 'Why do you need to find him before Monday, anyway?'

'Because,' he explained with desperate patience, 'when he went storming out of the office, he inadvertently took some plans with him, and they have to be in for tender on Monday!'

'Oh,' she said with infuriating indifference, 'well, I'm sorry, but I can't help you. Go and interrogate your sister; she probably knows where he is.'

'Don't be so stupid! If she knew where he was, I'd hardly be here, would I? Anyway, she'd be the last person to know!'

'Why would she?' she asked in confusion.

'Stop playing games, Justine! I know all about it!'

'All about what?'

His hard face registering distaste and disgust, he bit out, 'David left her a note.'

'So?'

'Oh, for pity's sake! Do we have to play this charade out to the bitter end? He left her a note saying you were going away together!'

'What?' Shocked out of her torpor, she lurched upright. 'Don't be so ridiculous! Why on earth would David and I go away together?'

'How the hell should I know? The idea of him wanting you as his mistress defies all comprehension!'

'His mistress? Don't be absurd! And don't be so bloody rude!'

'Rude? I'd like to exterminate you!' he ground out furiously. 'You are the most selfish, amoral little bitch it's ever been my misfortune to come across! Whatever you want, you take! People mean nothing to you! You cultivate them, then destroy them!'

Her eyes wide, her mouth practically hanging open, sheer astonishment held her rigid. She'd known he didn't like her, but to call her amoral...to say she destroyed people... 'Who have I ever destroyed?' she asked weakly.

'Oh, for God's sake! Don't tell me you don't remember that either! Katia!' he burst out. 'My sister! You callously accepted her hospitality, then set about ruining her reputation!'

'When?' she asked in genuine bewilderment. 'I've never done anything to Katia.'

His powerful hands bunched at his sides, he stalked across to the bed. 'Did you, or did you not, accept her invitation to stay in her hotel in Norway last summer?'

'Well, yes...'

'She asked you to vet the facilities and then, if you found them acceptable, to put her in touch with your contacts in the travel business. Yes?'

'Yes, but——'

'And then you systematically set about destroying her reputation——'

'I did no such thing!' she retorted, incensed. 'Who told you that? Katia? Because if she did, she's a bigger fool than even I took her for! She asked my opinion, and I gave it. Truthfully. How is that destroying her reputation?'

'You spread the word that her hotel was incapable of satisfying even the most undiscerning of guests!'

'I did not! My God, you do have a wonderful opinion of me!' Far more hurt than she would have believed possible by his scathing analysis of her character, she leaned tiredly back against the pillows. 'The hotel wasn't making money,' she explained slowly. 'Katia asked my advice. I gave it. I told her the truth because I was fond of her and David, and because I didn't want them to be hurt more than they had been. To run a hotel you need to be tough, efficient, full of energy! You also need to be ruthless! If the staff are no good, you have to fire them! Now David and Katia are very nice people, but neither of them are ruthless. They're both dreamers—so don't tell me they aren't,' she put in quickly when he opened his mouth, presumably to deny it, 'and you must have had windmills in your head if you thought her capable of running that sort of hotel! You're a businessman; would you have sent clients there? Wealthy, bored people with too much time and money? Oh, not all of them,' she qualified, seeing she was about to get a little homily on judging people by their wealth and status, 'but some of them. Most of them are perhaps nice, decent people, but not all. And people who pay the sort of money she was charging for holidays expect, rightly so, the best. To be pandered to, their every whim gratified, and neither Katia nor David could do that. At the first sign of dissatisfaction they panicked. It takes only one person to be rude to your sister, disparage her arrangements, and she dissolves in tears. Doesn't she?' she demanded. 'And that's why the hotel was losing money. Not from anything I said, or did, but because guests complained. Word spread that it was run inefficiently. I didn't spread the word, in fact I tried to promote it, against my better judgement perhaps, but I did try, and if she'd followed my advice and got a good manager in I would have promoted it! But she wouldn't, said she wanted to run it herself, so I advised her to lower her sights a bit; lower her prices, take in families, ordinary tourists, kindly middle-aged people wanting a lazy, interesting time, but she wouldn't. In the end, she was forced to sell, as I had warned her would happen. And as for ruining her, that's the height of absurdity! She actually made a profit on the sale! Didn't she? Oh, believe what you like,' she muttered; he would anyway, but, whatever he thought, it was true. Her motives hadn't been selfish, in fact she'd spent a great deal of time and trouble she could ill afford when she was trying to build up her own reputation.

'It wasn't a question of the money! It was a question of destroying her confidence in herself!'

'She doesn't *have* any confidence in herself!'

'No! Thanks to you!'

'Oh, don't be so wet! You're the one who destroys her confidence! The great high and mighty Kiel Lindstrom who can do anything and everything——'

'Which still doesn't alter the fact,' he overrode harshly, 'that the hotel idea was abandoned, forcing David to work at the boat-yard, which he hates and is totally unsuited for!'

'It didn't force him to anything! Katia's wealthy in her own right!'

'Yes! But just because you'd be quite happy to have men live off you doesn't mean Katia would! And, whatever I may think of David, he does at least have some pride! So where is he?'

'I don't know!' she yelled. 'How many more times must I tell you?'

'You have to know!' he shouted, then looked comically surprised at his own lack of control. Swinging away from her, he kicked moodily at the small upright chair in the corner. 'It's so easy for you, isn't it? You go on your way hurting and destroying people, little people who mean nothing to you. Well, Katia and John mean a very great deal to me.'

'John?' she queried tiredly. Who the hell was John?

'John Kendrick,' he explained impatiently. 'He owns the other half of the boat-yard that your uncle left to David—and all the time David stayed away,' he added aggrievedly, 'John made it pay. The minute David decides to take an interest, the whole thing falls apart at the seams!'

'Well, that's not my fault!'

'I didn't say it was!'

'Yes, you did, you said——'

'Oh, shut up!'

'A few more minutes only, Miss Hardesty, then your fiancé must leave.'

Swinging round in surprise, she stared at the little Chinese nurse. She hadn't even heard her come in! 'Fiancé?' she echoed in disbelief. 'Fiancé?'

With a comical look of surprise, the little nurse grinned at Kiel and backed out.

'Fiancé?' she repeated, turning her bewildered gaze on her tormentor.

'What else was I supposed to say?' he queried with a crotchety little shrug. 'I had Katia with me this morning, weeping and carrying on, and they wouldn't let me see you unless I was related.'

'Well, that fabrication was hardly likely to comfort her, was it? Not if she thinks I have designs on David. First her husband, then her brother. And I still can't believe that anyone in their right mind would give credence to the idea that I might be his mistress! She must have misunderstood the note.'

'She did not misunderstand the note! It stated quite clearly... Well, it...'

'Yes?' she asked sweetly.

Looking thoroughly disagreeable, he turned away and raked one hand through his thick and rather shaggy straw-coloured hair.

'It needs cutting,' she said without thinking.

Swinging back, and staring at her as though she were mad, he snapped, 'I know it needs cutting! I haven't had time! When I received John's call to tell me David had gone off with the plans, then Katia's hysterical interpretation, I was out testing a boat! I haven't had time to change, wash, or anything! By the time I'd found out about the crashed car and your whereabouts, I came straight here to meet her...'

'And between her weeping and wailing, you said the first thing that came into your head? I hope she didn't believe you,' she added maliciously.

'Don't be ridiculous. Anyway, Katia believes what she wants to believe. She's not like you, not strong, arrogant——'

'Oh, don't start that again. And I'm not in the least arrogant.'

'Hah! Next you'll be telling me you're a sweet-tempered clinging vine!'

'No, I wouldn't, because we both know I'm not, but I wouldn't have damned well wept and wailed if it had been my husband I thought had gone off with another woman.'

'No, you'd have strangled him, or the woman involved.'

'Not necessarily,' she said, rather miffed by his assumption. 'I'd probably have cut my losses. If men are unfaithful once, odds are they'll be unfaithful again.'

'And any man daft enough to fall in love with you would have to prove his undying devotion twenty-four hours a day,' he commented bitingly.

'Which is not something you'd ever have to worry about!' she snapped back. 'You don't even know the meaning of the word! And trading insults with me isn't going to find David! What exactly did his note say?'

'Oh, I don't know,' he denied wearily. 'Katia didn't actually give it to me to read, just said that he was going away for a bit, that he needed time to think. She wasn't making much sense, something about seeing you, that you didn't make a man feel threatened.'

'Well, I don't suppose I do,' she commented mildly. 'Men only presumably feel threatened if they care, and, believe me, David doesn't care, not in that way.'

'So why were you with him?'

'I don't know,' she admitted worriedly. 'I really don't know.'

'So we're back to where he might have gone.'

'Yes. I don't even remember seeing him,' she exclaimed, perplexed. 'As far as I'm aware I hadn't seen him since Christmas when we had a quick drink in the Cockney Pride. The last thing I remember is cooking Sunday lunch, so why on earth I would break that off and go dashing away with David I have no more idea than you. The time between one o'clock when I was cooking lunch and eleven at night when I was found lying beside David's car remains a complete blank.' She'd thought and thought, racking her brains to find an answer, a reason. Why? What extraordinary reason could she have had for rushing off with him in the middle of cooking lunch?

Sighing again, she stared morosely at her visitor, who was now leaning one broad shoulder against the window-frame and peering out between the slats. His thick green fisherman's sweater fitted smoothly across his massive back; the close-fitting twill trousers, salt-stained about the knee, emphasised his powerful thighs. Skier's thighs. Long, strong-muscled legs that would carry him effortlessly across long distances. The far-seeing eyes used to staring at distant horizons.

'So where would he go, Justine?' he continued with an air of great, enduring patience. 'Does he have a cottage anywhere? Yes?' he bit out hopefully when she looked suddenly thoughtful.

Her brow furrowed as she tried to capture an elusive memory, she murmured slowly, 'Madeira.'

'Madeira?' he exclaimed in disbelief. 'Why the bloody hell would he go to Madeira?'

Looking at him in exasperation, she snapped, 'People *do*, you know!'

'Quite possibly, I just meant that it didn't seem the sort of place David would go to. Not voluntarily anyway!'

'Well, it is! Or was,' she qualified. 'He used to borrow a friend's villa. Oh, ages ago, before he met Katia—he used to go there to paint...'

'Paint?'

'Yes, paint! And will you please stop repeating everything I say?' she exploded crossly.

'If you told things to me in a logical order, I wouldn't need to!'

'How the hell could I tell you in a logical order, when I've only just remembered?'

'A whole day wasted just because you were too bloody-minded... Where's the telephone?' he suddenly barked.

'I don't know, do I?'

Staring round him frustratedly as though expecting one to suddenly materialise, he strode over to the door. 'Stay there,' he rapped over his shoulder as he went out.

Where the hell did he think she was going with a broken wrist and concussion? Giving an aggrieved sigh, she closed her eyes. She had the most abominable headache, as though there were an army of elves inside her skull, all wielding large hammers, and her wrist hurt. Rest, the nurse had said; how the hell was she supposed to rest when the Norse god kept hassling her? And how gentle Katia came to have a brother so unlike herself she didn't know.

'So, we have established he has flown to Madeira,' he stated coldly as he thrust back through the door. 'His name was definitely on the passenger list for Sunday.'

'Oh, good,' she muttered sarcastically, 'I'm glad we've established something. Now you can go and book yourself a flight and leave me in peace. And on your way out, would you kindly tell the nurse that our engagement is terminated?' When he didn't answer, she widened her extraordinary eyes at him. He was staring at her assessingly, his head on one side. 'Why are you looking at me like that?' she burst out irritably.

'I was trying to decide if you had ever been gentle.'

'Why?'

Giving a long sigh, he admitted, 'I have no idea.'

Shaking her head in bewilderment, she added, 'Well, I hope you get your plans back and that Katia is ecstatically reunited with her darling husband, although why she's so agitated about it I can't for the life of me imagine. If he said he needed a few weeks to sort himself out, why is she so unwilling to give them? The plans aside, hassling him into coming back won't make him any more loving or amenable.'

'It had better,' he said grimly.

'Why?'

'Because she's pregnant.'

Staring at him in surprise, she felt her lips twitch.

'It isn't funny!' he snapped.

'No.'

'Then stop bloody laughing!'

'Dumped herself on you, has she?'

'Yes.'

'Ah.' No wonder he looked fraught. If he had to cope with Katia's fears, and maybe morning sickness, no wonder he looked thoroughly put out. 'Sick, is she?' she asked naughtily.

'Yes! You'd think she was the only woman on earth to ever get pregnant!'

'Women are often subject to odd fears and fancies,' she taunted softly, then grinned when he exploded.

'How the hell would you know? You've never been pregnant! Or have you?'

'No, I haven't.'

'Nor likely to be, the way you carry on,' he added disagreeably.

'Does David know?' she asked with a sudden frown. 'Is that why he went off?'

Looking startled, as though that was something he hadn't considered, his expression hardened, and a very vengeful light entered his dark green eyes. 'It had better not be.'

Wishing, not for the first time, that she could manage to keep her thoughts to herself when anywhere near this man, she hastily changed the subject. 'How many copies of the plans did he take?'

'What?'

'You said he went off with the plans, and well, I just thought it was a bit stupid leaving all copies of the same pla——' Breaking off, a rather naughty smile spread over her face as she correctly interpreted his expression. 'Oh-oh,' she taunted softly. 'Who didn't take copies, then? You?'

'No, it was not me!' he exploded harshly. 'And neither was it John's fault, not really. He'd only just finished putting the finishing touches to them, and before he had a chance to take photocopies David arrived.' Glaring at her as though it were all her fault, he rummaged in his back pocket and produced a grubby piece of paper and a pencil. 'Right. Address?'

'What?' she asked, confused.

'The address,' he said impatiently. 'I can't bloody find him without an address, can I?'

Staring at him, her face blank, she gave a comical little grimace. 'Ah.'

'Oh, God,' he said despairingly. 'You must have an address.'

'Well, I don't.'

'All right, the name of the chap who owns the villa then . . . Oh, for Pete's sake, you must know his name?'

For a moment, she actually felt quite sorry for him. He looked so utterly fed up.

'Have you been there?' he asked, grasping at the flimsiest straw.

'Once,' she admitted, 'but it was a long time ago, when David was going through one of his quixotic phases. I'd had a bad dose of flu and he took me out there to recuperate—and, before you ask, no, I do not remember where it is!'

'You must remember!' he exclaimed in disbelief.

'Well, I don't.' No doubt he was one of those infuriating people who only had to see a place once to have it indelibly imprinted on his memory.

'You said it was a villa.'

'It is.'

'Well, there you are, then.'

'What do you mean, there you are, then? Do you know how many villas there are on the island?' she exclaimed. 'Thousands of thousands! I can't just describe it and you'll find it! It will be like looking for a needle in a haystack!'

'Quite possibly,' he agreed urbanely, 'but with you along we at least have a chance of recognising the needle.'

'Oh, no, no way am I chasing off to Madeira——'

'Justine,' he broke in softly.

'No,' she denied stonily.

'Yes. The nurse said there was no earthly reason why you couldn't be discharged, as long as you take things easy.'

'Easy? Chasing off to Madeira comes under the heading of easy?'

'Certainly. Anyway, there isn't any choice. John needs those plans. He can't go rushing off and leave the yard unattended, which only leaves me. And you,' he added silkily. 'I don't have anything urgent on at the moment, and presumably we can get a flight to Lisbon quite easily, and then I imagine there's a shuttle service or something on to Funchal. I'll go and tell the nurse you're ready to leave——'

'I am not ready to leave!' she stormed.

With a very nasty smile, he said softly, 'Yes, you are. We'll go to your flat to pack and then we'll go to my house near Southampton——'

'No,' she said positively. 'What marvellous God-given right do you think you have to make me dash off to Madeira?'

Leaning over the end of the bed, he gave another imitation of the Cheshire cat. 'Because you owe them.'

'Owe them?' she asked in astonishment. 'Owe them what?'

'Don't you feel even slightly morally obliged? You successfully ruined their hotel business so that David was forced into the yard, which he hates and has no interest in——'

'I did not!'

'. . . and then won't lift a finger to save it from losing a very lucrative contract.'

'I did not ruin their hotel business! They were being too ambitious and I told them so! I'm not his damned keeper! David's a grown man, for goodness' sake; if he can't get his act together at his age... Apart from which, he's not even a member of my family! Not a blood relation, anyway!'

'Don't split hairs. However remote the connection, the fact remains he took papers that didn't belong to him.'

'But he didn't take them on purpose, you said so...'

'What difference does that make? And even if you don't owe it to him, what about Margaret? Did she split hairs when she took you in when your parents died?'

'Oh, damn you, get out of here!'

Giving her a triumphant glance, he taunted over his shoulder as he strode to the door, 'I'll send the nurse in. Don't be too long, will you? And don't try to disappear, because I'd find you. Believe me, I'd find you.'

Justine didn't doubt him for a moment. Leaning weakly back against the pillows, she glared after him. Mind, he'd been right about Aunt Margaret; if she didn't help find her precious David, she'd never hear the last of it. After the death of her parents fifteen years before, in an air show crash, she'd gone to live with her mother's brother, Tom Naughton, who had only recently married Margaret and taken on her young son, David, who had then been fourteen, two years older than herself. So from his single state he'd not only gained a wife, but two children as well. Sadly, he himself had died two years later, leaving Margaret to bring up the children on her own. It couldn't have been easy for her, Justine appreciated that, and she had fed and clothed her, but love and understanding had seemed in very short supply, and she found it hard now to summon up any affection for the woman who had lavished all her maternal feelings on her son.

Kiel had called her hard, aggressive, but she wasn't, not really. Not inside. Inside, she was still the vulnerable child who had been so starved of affection, approbation; and there still was that need for approval, she supposed, or why else did she work so hard to be a success? The circumstances of her youth had forced her to be strong or be utterly crushed by her aunt's indifference to her needs, and now, she thought rather sadly, her earlier pretence of being strong seemed to have become reality. Had her parents not died she would probably have been very different. A clinging vine? No, she doubted she'd ever have been that, but she might have been softer, more feminine. And that's what hurts, isn't it, Justine? Being called unfeminine. But when you had to fight for every inch of space, fight to make something of yourself, wasn't it to be expected that you would lose something along the way? And was it really unfeminine to be proud of your achievements? Of standing on your own two feet and winning? And for a moment, for one brief moment, before she forced herself back under control, she felt a wave of self-pity wash over her. No fond parent to visit her, tell her it was OK. No siblings to tease her, write on her cast. Fool, she scolded herself, didn't your years with Aunt Margaret teach you the folly of self-pity?

Pulling a face of disgust for her weakness, she pushed the bitter memories to the back of her mind and considered her options. She couldn't fulfil her own obligations with her wrist in plaster—then she gave a wry smile. That was the understatement of the year; whoever heard of a golfer playing with a broken wrist? Damn, she'd been due to play in a tournament in Normandy at the end of the week—now she'd have to find someone to take her place. Who? Peter? His wife *would* be pleased if she sent him chasing off to France at a moment's notice—but then maybe his wife could go with him? Someone had to go, and Peter was the obvious choice. Not only could he play the course, he could also vet the hotel, and if it was suitable, and she thought it probably would be, that was another hotel she could add to her list of exclusive golf resorts. The company was only small as yet, but doing very nicely, thank you. They had all their bookings done for this year... Her secretary,

Lorraine, could handle any cancellations, or last-minute bookings, so yes, Peter to vet the French hotel for next year's list—she'd have to pay for his wife of course, but still... Her mouth pursed, she continued to work out all viable options.

'Aren't you ready yet?' Kiel demanded angrily.

'What? No, I'm not! Honestly, Kiel, this whole thing's dumb! Madeira's a big place...'

'Which means the sooner we get going, the sooner we can begin to search!'

Grumbling irritably, she pushed back the covers. 'I seem to have spent my whole life bailing David out of trouble; I should really leave him to stand on his own two feet!' But if Katia was pregnant, and the yard needed this contract... Oh, knickers, having a conscience was a damnable nuisance. If she didn't help find the plans, and David, she wouldn't be able to stop worrying about it, despite Kiel's opinion that she was hard and unfeeling. And trust Margaret to disappear off to Australia just when she was needed. Damn woman had probably done it on purpose.

CHAPTER TWO

'WELL, go on, then, go away! I'm not getting dressed with you here!'

With another look of irritation, Kiel went out, holding the door politely for the nurse to enter.

'This is not a good idea,' Justine told her darkly.

'Want me to tell him to come back tomorrow?' the nurse teased.

'Yes!'

'It wouldn't work...'

'So tell me something I don't know! And aren't I supposed to see the doctor before I'm discharged so summarily?'

'Doctor says it's all right...'

'Oh, he would,' she said disgustedly. 'I'm ill, dammit!'

Chuckling, the nurse handed her two white pills.

'What are these?'

'Painkillers. Come on, wash them down.' Handing Justine a glass of water, she went to collect her clothes from the locker.

After struggling into the jeans and sweater that she had been wearing at the time of the accident, a process which thoroughly exhausted her, she sank limply down on the side of the bed while the nurse knelt to fit her shoes on to her feet.

'I don't know why you're in such a bad mood; I would be most happy to be whisked off by that hunk.'

'Hunk?' Justine derided. 'The man's a megalomaniac, and if you had any idea what he intends doing you wouldn't be so enamoured of him either.'

'What?' she asked, her eyes alight with interest.

'Dragging me off to Madeira!'

'Lucky you.'

'Lucky me? In my state of health?'

'You'll be all right. He looks the sort to cherish women.'

'Not this one, he doesn't. He's just as likely to push me off a precipice!' Taking the bag that the nurse held out, and the bottle of painkillers, she considered the nurse's words with a sense of disbelief. Cherish women? Kiel? She had to be joking! He wouldn't even know where to start.

When he came back in at the nurse's urging, his face still set in a scowl, she tried to view him dispassionately. Did he look the sort to cherish women? No, she decided, he didn't. He looked impatient, arrogant, hard.

'Ready?'

'No.' Giving him a sour glance, she got to her feet. With a little sniff, she preceded him from the room.

Pausing at the reception desk, she took the blue appointment card they gave her.

'Come back in two weeks to have the plaster checked. If you get any dizziness or nausea, come back or see your own doctor. Don't drive...oh, sorry, you can't, can you?' the nurse asked as she eyed the plaster cast. The smile she gave Kiel was a great deal warmer than the one she gave Justine.

With another sniff, she accompanied Kiel out to his car. Glancing disagreeably at the long, elegant lines in racing green—no doubt chosen to match his eyes, she thought cynically—she climbed in. Refusing his offer of help with the seatbelt, she leaned back and wondered if she'd gone completely round the bend.

His hand on the ignition key, he said softly, 'We can do this the easy way, or we can do it the hard way. Your temper I can match insult for insult—and I will win. I need your help, which you can give grudgingly, or generously, but make no mistake, Justine, your help I am going to have.' Without waiting for her to answer, he fired the engine.

Bastard, she thought mutinously. She'd have given her help more than generously if he'd been understanding, kind; or at least tried to consider her feelings in all this, but he hadn't. He hadn't even asked her how she felt. Not once. Although he was right about one thing: he would win. He always did, and if she tried to balk him at every turn she'd end up a nervous, exhausted wreck. But oh, how it galled her to give in to this man.

It only took a few minutes to get to her flat, and as she pushed through into the kitchen-diner she halted in confusion. She had fully expected the kitchen to show signs of abandoned preparations for dinner, and it didn't, it was spotless. Frowning, she turned to survey the lounge area.

'What's the matter?' he asked shortly.

Turning towards him, she explained haltingly, 'Why would I only remember cooking lunch? If I cleared away, as I presumably must have done, why don't I remember that?'

'How should I know? I'm not a doctor. Can we get on now, please? And don't forget your passport.'

Barely listening to him, her mind still on the puzzle of the tidy flat, she walked into the bedroom. Collecting her small suitcase from the cupboard, she threw some things into it and went back to the lounge.

'Right. Gas off? Electricity?'

'What? Oh, no, I'll do it now. I also have to make some phone calls...'

'You can make them from my house.'

'No, I can't! I have to make them now.' Plumping down by the phone, ignoring Kiel's sigh of impatience, she picked up the receiver, and, listening to make sure she had a dialling tone, laid it down and proceeded to punch out Peter's number. Because Peter had a large old house, with plenty of room, they had turned his front room into their office, and so far it had worked very well. Explaining quickly, she thanked God for Peter's quick grasp of essentials.

'Can I leave it all to you? Yes, I should be back in a few days; no, the details are all in the file. OK, thanks, I should see you some time next week. I'll keep in touch. OK, bye.'

Replacing the receiver, she gave Kiel an absent smile while her mind went over anything she might have forgotten.

'Ready now?' he asked sarcastically.

Giving a long sigh, she nodded. 'I suppose.'

Feeling thoroughly out of sorts with him and the world in general, a mood that didn't improve during the drive to his home, she tried to cudgel her brain into remembrance of events prior to her accident, but it remained infuriatingly blank. She then switched her mind to memories of Madeira, only they seemed equally hazy. How in heaven was she to find a villa on an island covered in them? Not that she *actually* had to go. She didn't *have* to allow him to browbeat her. So why was she? Guilt? For, although Kiel's accusations that she had ruined the hotel business weren't true, she hadn't been as helpful as she might have been. Hadn't been as sympathetic, and might not the reason that she had been so vociferous in her own defence be because there had been a modicum of truth in his words? The trouble was, both David and Katia always made her feel so impatient; they wouldn't get on with life! They waited around for direction, and that just wasn't her way! It wasn't Kiel's either. So why was he accusing her of the very behaviour he himself used? Guilt of his own? Turning her head, she stared at his hard-etched profile. No, she thought with an inward sigh, he would never blame himself when there was someone else to load it on.

When he braked to a halt in a showy flourish that sprayed gravel everywhere, she gave him a look of disdain, but it was herself who looked away first on encountering his blank green stare. When he helped her from the car, she stared in astonishment at the funny little house, then gave an amused grunt of laughter, the first sign of humour she had evinced since the accident. Was it a joke? she wondered. Kiel was one of the largest men she knew, and this house had to be the smallest. Dark beams criss-crossed the front, not replicas, she decided, but the genuine article. Tudor, probably, and trust Kiel to own what was no doubt the only genuine private Tudor dwelling in the whole world. It seemed to be tilted drunkenly to one side, making her feel giddy. In normal circumstances, she would have been delighted at the chance to stay here, and if it hadn't belonged to Kiel she would have been now.

When the door was flung open to reveal a middle-aged woman who was as wide as she was high, her grey hair screwed up into an untidy bun, Justine decided to let events take their course. She just didn't have the energy for any more arguments and discussions.

'Just in time for dinner,' the woman exclaimed in satisfaction. Giving Justine a cluck of sympathy, she took the suitcase from Kiel and ushered them both indoors. Kiel had to duck his head quite severely to get through the door and she wondered again why someone so tall should buy a house that was so tiny.

When Justine had tidied herself as best she could in the small cloakroom, she joined Kiel in the dining-room. Her plaster cast resting on the table, she slowly drank her soup. When that was replaced by a fluffy omelette, she did her best to do it justice, but, after managing only a few mouthfuls, she put down her fork.

'Not hungry?' Kiel asked quietly.

Shaking her head, she then winced as pain shot through it.

'Headache?'

'Mm, and double vision, and my arm aches, and I feel fretful, and irritable, and tired.'

'Poor Justine,' he mocked solemnly. 'Melly?' he shouted, and, when the housekeeper bustled in, he added, 'Show Justine to her room, will you? She's tired.'

'Well, of course she is,' Melly insisted strongly. 'She's got concussion!'

Her championship took both Justine and Kiel by surprise; they looked at each other in astonishment, and she could have sworn that just for a moment Kiel's lips twitched.

'Come on, ducks, don't take no notice of him. If it was him with concussion and a broken arm, we'd never hear the last of it.'

'Help is hard to come by,' he murmured blandly, and Justine gave a tired smile. So the wretched man did have a sense of humour.

Getting awkwardly to her feet, she accompanied Melly up the funny bent little staircase, but found she was too tired to really take in the décor or quaint architecture. Her vision had developed an alarming tendency to go in and out of focus and she was more than thankful to enter the bedroom Melly showed her and collapse on to the bed.

'Can you manage, dear?'

'Yes, thanks. I'm beginning to get quite adept.' Which wasn't strictly true, but seemed easier to say than ask for help.

When Melly had kindly removed her nightdress and dressing-gown from her case and gone, she just sat for a few minutes and stared blankly at the wall while trying to summon up the energy to get undressed. What a day!

Kicking off her shoes, she struggled out of her jeans and tossed them over the chair. It was when it came to removing the jumper that her troubles began, for she couldn't get it over the plaster cast.

'Oh, come on, Justine, you got it on, so you must be able to get it off!' Slumping tiredly back on the bed, her sweater tangled round one arm, she contemplated sleeping as she was in bra and pants, and the wretched jumper, but her bra seemed to rub against bruises she hadn't known she'd got until she had dressed in the hospital. Perhaps if she just took off her bra? Her brain felt all scrambled up, incapable of reasoning rationally, and when she finally managed to unhook it she threw it untidily on the floor in a burst of temper and resentment. Crawling under the covers, she fell almost instantly asleep.

She wasn't sure what woke her the next morning, a small noise, or just an awareness of being watched. Whatever it was, she reluctantly unglued her lashes, then stared blankly up at Kiel.

'Teddy substitute?' he enquired almost pleasantly.

'What?' She frowned, uncomprehending, until he nodded towards the jumper bundled up against her chest. Lowering her eyes to it, she grimaced. 'No, I couldn't get it off.'

When he put out his hand, she reluctantly dragged herself upright. Clutching both woolly and duvet to her nakedness, she extended her plastered wrist.

With a humorous glance that made her want to hit him, he eased the jumper off without any trouble at all.

'Thank you,' she said grudgingly.

'Pleasure. I came to see if you wanted some breakfast; you didn't eat any dinner last night.'

'Mm, thank you. I'll come down,' she mumbled.
For some extraordinary reason, she felt shy of him,
which annoyed her. She'd never been shy in her life.
Perhaps it was because he was in her bedroom, and
she was virtually naked.

'Can you manage?' he asked softly, and he
sounded as though he was trying very hard not to
laugh.

Giving him a suspicious glance, she nodded. 'Yes,
thank you.'

'Very well, I'll tell Melly you'll be down shortly.'

When he'd gone, she stared thoughtfully at the
closed door. Why was he being so helpful all of a
sudden? He'd never been helpful, or even polite, in
the three years she'd known him. So why now? Unable to come up with an answer, she got out of bed
and padded into the bathroom.

Awkwardly washing and cleaning her teeth, she
then discovered just the first of another set of problems that were about to beset her. She couldn't put
her hair up one-handed, nor could she tie it back.
The plaster cast left only the tips of her fingers free,
and, struggle as she might, she couldn't grasp anything. She hated leaving her hair loose; it looked untidy, and, being fine, flew everywhere at the slightest
provocation. She was quite unaware that the shining
curtain presented an almost unbearable temptation
for any male lucky enough to see it in all its shining
glory. Not that many people were allowed to see it
so—it was usually ruthlessly piled on top of her head

and securely clipped in place. With a sigh, she went back to the bedroom, only to discover the next of her problems. While it had been comparatively easy to unclip her bra one-handed, it was impossible to put it on that way. Throwing it into her case in disgust, she pulled out a loose sweater. Struggling into clean jeans, and pushing her feet into soft leather moccasins, she went out and down the crooked little staircase. Running her hand over the rough plaster walls, she wondered absently how many centuries of people had done just that. Maybe her hand touched the exact same spot as a Tudor lady's or gentleman's, then she smiled faintly at her romanticism, which was so unlike her. She was usually a very practical, down-to-earth girl, who very rarely indulged in fancy. Reaching the hall, she smiled as Melly came out of what was presumably the kitchen carrying a coffee-pot.

'Morning, ducks, sleep well?' Without waiting for an answer, she continued, 'Heard you coming; how do you feel this morning?'

'Not too bad, thank you, Melly,' then, giving a rueful little smile, apologised, 'I'm sorry if I was rude last night.'

'Lord love you!' she exclaimed. 'Feeling pretty rotten, weren't you? Besides, it's all water off a duck's back to me. After his lordship, anybody else's temper seems mild.'

'Thank you for the testimonial,' Kiel approved as he emerged from the dining-room. 'However, there is no need to warn Justine; she's already formed her own opinion of my character.'

Grinning cheekily at him, Melly waved the coffee-pot under his nose. 'If you're looking for the coffee, it's here.'

'Here is not where I want it,' he drawled, and, when Melly pulled a face and took it into the dining-room, he turned his attention to Justine.

'How do you feel?'

'Exasperated,' she informed him. 'I've just discovered that I can't wear half the clothes I brought with me.' When he raised his eyebrows in query, she explained, 'I can't do up buttons, hooks, or zips one-handed.'

'Oh.' Allowing his eyes to move from the soft fall of hair down to her chest, almost as though he could see she wasn't wearing a bra, he grinned. 'I would offer to act as lady's maid, only——'

'Quite,' she said hastily. She was already knocked off balance by his glance, and his teasing seemed more than she felt able to cope with. With a mean-ingless smile, she edged past him.

'I have to go out for a while,' he continued. 'Please use the house as your own. Do you need anything?'

Unable to resist, she smiled at him over her shoul-der. 'Hemlock?' When he laughed, she shook her head. 'No, thank you.'

Tucking into the eggs and bacon that Melly placed before her, all cut up in little pieces as though for a child, she smiled her thanks. When she'd finished, she poured herself coffee, then leaned back in her chair and thought about Kiel. What had he meant about forming an opinion? His words seemed to imply that she'd misjudged him in some way, or he thought she had. Frowning thoughtfully, she considered all she knew about him, which admittedly wasn't much, but she certainly wasn't wrong about the arrogance, or his being domineering. Although, she supposed, to be fair, being domineering wasn't exactly a dislikeable trait, unless carried to extremes; she was a bit domineering herself. Presumably he got just as impatient with fools as she did. And to be honest, he'd been quite nice that morning. The trouble was, did she want him to be nice? If he was nice, she'd have to be nice back, and she wasn't sure she wanted to be. Or forgive him for the insults he'd hurled in the hospital.

On the other hand... With a wry smile, she stirred sugar into her coffee. And if they hadn't got off to such a bad start the first time they'd met at David and Katia's engagement party, maybe they would even have become friends. But they had got off to a bad start. They'd met rather violently in the car park outside the hall. He'd backed his car into hers, and instead of waiting to find out why, or how, he'd managed to do such a damned fool thing, she'd lost her temper and hadn't allowed him to explain. She'd found out later, not from him, that a child had been coming down the hill, out of control on a bike, and if he hadn't reversed at speed the child would have hit his car instead of the hedge, and no doubt been killed. She'd seen none of the drama because she'd been too busy shouting at him. A rueful curve to her mouth, she sipped her coffee—they'd been shouting at each other ever since. He'd written her off as insensitive and selfish, and she'd written him off as a boor. He hadn't allowed her to apologise when she had found out about the child, just given her a withering glance and walked off. Oh, well.

Finishing her coffee, she wandered through to the lounge. Perching on the window-seat beneath the double casement windows that gave on to the garden, she stared round her, and her interest perked up as she noticed the pictures lining the walls. Old prints for the most part, depicting the Tudor period. Line drawings of faces, interesting, weathered, their eyes holding knowledge of another age, another time.

When Melly bustled in, Justine smiled at her, then, indicating the pictures, added, 'They're beautiful.'

'Yes, they are. Spends ages he does, searching them out. Junk shops, antiques, jumble sales.'

Surprised, Justine tried to imagine the adventurous-looking Kiel poking around in junk shops, and failed miserably.

'Quite a hobby of his,' Melly continued. 'Fanatical, you might say. Hears about one and off he goes.' Plumping up cushions and rearranging the plants on the mantelshelf as she spoke, as though it were a sin to be idle, she straightened the cretonne cover on the sofa, and patted it invitingly. 'Now you just come and put your feet up for a bit; you'll be doing enough dashing about if I know Kiel. Make the most of a rest now.'

Amused, Justine did as she was told.

'Want some advice?' Melly asked as she came to stand at the foot of the sofa.

'You said that as though you're going to give me some whether I want it or not,' she replied wryly.

'I am,' Melly grinned. 'If you want to emerge in one piece, don't prod his temper, otherwise you might find you have a tiger by the tail. And don't fall in love with him. It won't do you a bit of good.'

'Thank you, Melly,' she returned drily, 'I'll try to remember.'

'Think I'm joking, don't you? Well, I'm not.' Moving away, she began straightening pictures that didn't need straightening. Running one finger along the highly polished sideboard, and examining it for traces of dust, she added with a vague air that was extremely suspect, 'I've seen them all, you know, young girls throwing themselves at him, older women, the plain, the pretty...'

'My, my, he does have a busy time, doesn't he?' Justine mocked with mild sarcasm, then hastily straightened her face when Melly turned to give her a penetrating glance.

'You may mock, my girl, but don't come running to me when you get hurt.'

'I won't,' she promised. A promise she considered herself quite safe in making. She could conceive of there being no likelihood whatsoever of her falling in love with Kiel Lindstrom, and the thought of an army of women throwing themselves at his feet only made her smile.

'Well, don't say I didn't warn you,' Melly said portentously as she went out.

'I won't,' she denied softly. Unfortunately, Melly's dire warnings set her speculating, and, relaxing back on the sofa, she contemplated Kiel's reaction if she suddenly declared her undying devotion. Horror? Shock? Amusement? With a little giggle, she wondered idly what he might look for in a woman. Obviously none to date had captured that hard heart. Did he even want it captured? In the hospital, it had been difficult to imagine a softer side to him, and quite easy to believe that domestic pursuits would bore him, but here, in his own home, he seemed more relaxed, gentler...

'What's amusing you?' the object of her thoughts asked as he came into the room.

'Mm? Oh, hello, nothing much, just thoughts. What's this?' she asked in surprise as he tossed a parcel into her lap.

'Open it and find out,' he instructed mildly as he came to perch on the sofa arm.

Tearing open the wrapper, she stared dumbfounded at the contents. An expensive knitted cotton tracksuit in lavender. Lifting both items out, she lay them across her lap.

'To match your eyes,' he observed easily, then smiled in satisfaction when she looked at him.

'But why?' she asked, bewildered.

'Because they don't have any zips, buttons, or hooks,' he explained, as though it were the most reasonable thing in the world and she was a fool for not understanding.

'But I can't take this.'

'Why?'

'Well, because,' she said lamely.

'Oh, an excellent reason,' he mocked. 'Look on it as payment for services rendered.'

'But I haven't rendered any yet.' Staring at him, her eyes troubled, she said honestly, 'And it's extremely doubtful I ever will. You still seem to be labouring under the notion that I will instantly remember all when we get to Madeira, and I won't.'

'You might.'

'And then again I might not!' she said in exasperation. 'I don't know why you're being so stubborn. It's nearly ten years since I was there.'

With a little shrug, he got to his feet in one lazy movement. 'Ten years is not so long.'

'Maybe not,' she agreed helplessly, 'if I hadn't done anything else in between. But I have. I've been to so many different places since then, and all I can remember of that time is a crazy jumble of images, impressions, nothing concrete at all.'

Coming to perch beside her on the couch, he took her hand in his, and she stared rather bemusedly at the large palm engulfing her own. It felt warm, and, for some silly reason, made her feel secure.

'You're the only hope I have, Justine. I know it's asking a lot, but Naughton's need that order, desperately. All I'm asking is that you try.'

Her shoulders slumping tiredly, she nodded. She didn't honestly think it would do any good.

'We'll be leaving in about ten minutes. Melly will repack your case, so all you have to do is rest.' Removing the tracksuit from her lap, he got up and went out.

Left alone with her thoughts, she tried to focus her mind, conjure up something more concrete than a tiny bay dotted with fishing-boats and red-roofed villas. She could remember banana plantations; and she had a vague recollection of an extinct volcano, but that was all really, except that it had been very hilly. She remembered Funchal, the capital, but the villa hadn't been near there. With a despondent sigh, she leaned back again. She could hear Kiel talking to Melly in the kitchen, not the words, just the murmur of their voices. What a very odd man he was. One minute jumping down her throat, and the next, buying her a tracksuit.

Hearing the doorbell ring, she turned her head curiously, thankful for something to take her mind off her troubled thoughts. She heard Kiel's voice raised in exasperation, then recognised Katia's tearful tones. Oh, hell, that was all she needed, Katia weeping and wailing all over her. And that's not very charitable, she scolded herself; that knock on the head hasn't improved your nature one iota.

When the door opened, she stiffened, then relaxed limply back. Arguing with Katia wouldn't solve anything and would probably only make her head ache. Her eyes wary as she stared at the small, dark-haired girl, she greeted her quietly, 'Hello, Katia.' Kiel was standing behind her, one large hand resting protectively on her shoulder. Katia's rather sulky mouth was set in a pout, her eyes sparkling with temper and a hint of tears as she stared rudely at Justine.

'What have you done with David?' she asked bluntly. 'Where is he?'

'I don't know,' Justine denied tiredly. 'Truly, Katia, if I did, I'd tell you.'

'No, you would not!' she snapped. Shrugging off Kiel's hand, she advanced into the room. 'He said to me, no good is it asking Justine, she won't tell.'

Oh, hell, why on earth would David say that? Justine wondered drearily. Trust him to make a mess of everything—and drag her into it. 'I can't tell, because I don't know,' she explained as patiently as possible. 'I don't remember anything. If I did, I'd say so.'

'No, you would not! Well, I come to Madeira too...'

'Oh, no, you won't!' Kiel put in hastily. 'You will stay here.'

'No!' she yelled, swinging round to face him. 'He is mine, you think she will have him, keep him and then I will forget! Well, I won't! He is mine, and that, that—person will not have my David. You have never liked him, never wanted for me to marry with him——'

'That's not true——'

'Yes! Is true! You have never liked him. You say he is lazy, stupid——'

'I never said any such thing!' Grasping her by the shoulders, he steered her out into the kitchen, but Justine could clearly hear her tearful remonstrations and Kiel's short replies.

When he returned to the lounge, his face was set in harsh, angry lines, much as it had been in the hospital, and Justine sighed. So much for better relations.

'She's wrong,' she said quietly. 'I have only normal cousinly fondness for David, and I can't for the life of me understand why he's pretending otherwise.' Examining his face and finding not one atom of softening, she blew her breath out in exasperation. He was staring at her as though she were some unsavoury specimen pinned under a microscope—and it hurt.

'We'll go now,' he said abruptly. 'Melly's put your things in the car. Do you have your passport?'

'Yes,' she admitted defeatedly. Getting to her feet, she preceded him out to the car.

* * *

The drive to Heathrow was made in silence. Justine didn't feel like making conversation, and Kiel certainly didn't look as though he wished to indulge in small talk. He put the car in the long-stay car park, then, collecting both bags, he marched off across the overpass leaving Justine to trail after him. Hitching her bag more comfortably over her shoulder, making sure her passport was within easy reach, she followed his tall striding figure. Not once did he look back to see if she was there, and she pulled a little face. You can be just too confident, she told him silently. And I shall expect a damned apology from you, my lad, when—if—we find David and get this mess sorted out.

Their flight was just being called when they entered the departure-lounge, and, as though remembering her for the first time, he halted and took her arm. Looking down into her set face, he gave a long sigh. 'Oh, come on,' he encouraged wearily. 'It's your own fault, you know. You should have left David alone.'

'I didn't touch him! How many more times do I have to say it? If I wanted an affair, which I don't,' she denied strenuously, 'it certainly wouldn't be with my own cousin!'

Ignoring her petulance, he urged her towards the boarding ramp. Managing a half-smile for the stewardess, she took a window-seat, and as he settled himself beside her she gazed blindly out the window. She felt obscurely hurt and unhappy, and was far too aware of his massive bulk beside her. Of the strong, blunt-fingered hands resting easily on his knees, which were too close to her own. Moving her legs rather ostentatiously away, she sighed. Why did life have to get so complicated? When he leaned across her, she flinched away.

'Oh, for goodness' sake!' he growled, his face so close that she could see every golden eyelash. 'I was only going to do your seatbelt up.'

'Oh. Well, all right, then,' she muttered, feeling an absolute fool.

'And you can stop sulking.'

'I wasn't. I just don't like being accused of something without being given a chance to defend myself. I feel out of sorts, my arm aches, and I just want to be left alone,' she added childishly. 'No one seems to consider my feelings in all this. I've been dragged off against my will; had no chance to go into the office; all I had time for was a hurried telephone call...' When he gave a snort of what sounded suspiciously like laughter, she turned on him crossly. 'And if you're going to start being reasonable again I think I might hit you! There is nothing more irritating than someone being nice and reasonable when all you want is a good slanging match—especially when that person has practically accused you of being a home-wrecker!'

'Still want one?' he asked humorously.

'No, I think I'm too tired. Why? Would you have indulged me if I had?'

'Probably not; like you, I sometimes like to be perverse.'

'Only sometimes?' she asked in astonishment. That wasn't the impression she had received.

'Mm, only sometimes. Tell me what you meant about David's painting,' he encouraged. 'You said that was why he used the villa.'

Fighting her own internal battle with her temper, she finally shrugged. 'I don't know if he still paints,' she muttered grudgingly, 'but he used to do it quite a lot. Seascapes mostly—he loved the sea, which makes it even more odd that he doesn't like sailing. He was very good,' she added reminiscently, and he had been. The only thing he had really excelled at. 'It always seems so sad,' she murmured half to herself, 'that when people have such a God-given talent they don't use it.'

'Mm. And what God-given talent do you have?' he asked rather sardonically.

'Me? Oh, hell, I don't know.' Thinking about it, a gleam of humour lit her lovely eyes, and with a provocative glance at him from under her lashes she teased, 'I just drive men insane.' She expected him to laugh, join in the joke, because that was what it was intended to be, only he didn't. He looked away, leaned back and closed his eyes. Rather nonplussed, she turned back to the window, her face thoughtful. As far as she was aware she'd never driven any man wild in her life, nor did she think she was ever likely to, although that didn't seem to be the interpretation Kiel had put on her words. She supposed drearily that he'd thought she was referring to David. Well, she was too tired to go through it all again, and, with a mental shrug, she too leaned back and closed her eyes.

When they landed, and began to file out, Justine didn't miss the warm smile the air hostess gave Kiel, just as she had during the flight. She'd seemed to spend an inordinate amount of time asking him if he was comfortable, needed anything. Snorting rudely as she passed her, which earned her a look of astonishment, Justine suddenly, unexpectedly grinned. She knew her behaviour stemmed from sour grapes, and maybe if she'd smiled at Kiel he might have smiled back as he had at the hostess, a warm crinkly sort of smile. Although why she should want him to smile at her she had no clear idea, and because of her lack of attention she stumbled on the last step of the ramp.

'Are you all right?' he asked in concern.

'Yes, just tired I think, although how sitting down for a couple of hours doing nothing can be tiring I don't quite know.' And she was tired, even though that wasn't the reason she'd stumbled. Not that she was about to tell him that. Tucking her hand into his arm, she naughtily leaned more heavily than she needed until he stopped abruptly and looked down into her face, his eyes full of amusement.

'Overdoing it a bit, am I?' she queried humorously.

'Just a touch, I think,' he said sardonically.

With a little laugh, she accompanied him through into the modern lounge for transit passengers, then sat and waited while Kiel went to make enquiries about a flight to Madeira. Fortunately they didn't have to wait very long, and it was only a few minutes later that they were walking across the tarmac to board the little local plane.

When they alighted in Madeira, Justine began to feel more cheerful. Looking round curiously at the surrounding hills that seemed to dwarf them, then at the very short length of the runway, she wondered fleetingly how on earth the plane had managed to land in such a small place.

'Bring back any memories?' he asked quietly.

'Not really,' she sighed. 'Although it was dark when I arrived before.'

She obediently climbed the narrow stairs at his urging, and they joined the queue to have their passports stamped.

'Where are we going?' she asked curiously as he led her outside to a waiting taxi.

'Machico. It's the second largest town on the island, nearer to the airport than Funchal; it seemed reasonable to start there.'

As they zoomed up the exit ramp, the force of the acceleration threw them both backwards into a tangled heap.

'Trust you to find a driver who thinks he's Fangio,' she gasped. Grabbing his arm in an effort to keep her balance, she turned to look at him and found his face a great deal closer than she had expected. Staring into sea-green eyes, she saw her reflection dancing in their depths, and hastily righted herself before muttering an apology. Suddenly he was no longer a reluctant companion, someone she was forced to travel with, but a warm male animal and all that that entailed. She stupidly hadn't considered that when she'd agreed to come.

Edging away, she stared out the window, and she could have passed a herd of wild elephants and not seen them. She knew he was watching her, could feel his gaze on her, probably puzzled by her reaction, or over-reaction, she qualified to herself, which was all it had been. She was just being stupid, no doubt due to the concussion. Don't fall in love with him, Melly had said. Well, she wouldn't, there was no danger of that, but being aware of his masculinity, that was a horse of a very different colour.

CHAPTER THREE

'SEE anything familiar?' Kiel asked.

'No,' Justine denied huskily, but that was because she wasn't looking, only she could hardly tell him that. 'Did you book us in somewhere?'

'Mm, the Dom Pedro, but don't ask me where it is or what it's like, because I have no idea. And don't ask me to interpret for you either,' he added with a grin, 'because neither do I speak Portuguese. However, I expect we'll get by.'

'Yes.' Nice to be so confident; no doubt he always got by, either by sheer weight of personality or the charm he was beginning to display from time to time... Justine was forced to abandon her unprofitable thoughts as they screeched round yet another bend. 'I'll be glad when we arrive—if we arrive,' she added morosely as she fought to keep her injured arm from violent contact with the seat in front.

'Feeling rough?' he asked, and he sounded genuinely concerned, which she supposed he was; he'd look a bit stupid if she died on him.

'A bit. I'll be all right when I'm stationary.' In truth her head was beginning to pound again, and she felt slightly sick. Giving him a wan smile, that told him a great deal more of how she was feeling than she supposed, she caught a glimpse of blue sea over his shoulder, and a brief memory surfaced. Leaning forward to get a better view, she forgot for a moment her earlier awareness of him. Her hand on his knee to balance herself, her long hair tangling against his grey V-necked sweater, she didn't notice that his thigh muscles tensed, or that he took a swift indrawn breath. Concentrating on the view, she frowned.

'Remember something?'

'I'm not sure,' she began slowly. 'The curve of the bay perhaps.'

'Don't force it,' he instructed softly. 'Let it come naturally.'

With a little nod, she leaned back in her seat and stared at the hotel that rose bizarrely before them. It looked extremely out of place among all the tiny red-roofed villas; progress, she supposed. Yet surely, such a large hotel, if she had seen it before, should have remained in her memory.

'*Obrigada,*' she murmured unthinkingly as the taxi driver opened the door for her.

'You speak Portuguese!' Kiel accused. 'Although I don't know why I should be surprised; you probably speak any number of languages, travelling as you do.'

'Some,' she admitted, 'although not Portuguese, or only a word or two. Funny, I wasn't consciously aware that I remembered any.'

Following Kiel into the hotel, she stared round her curiously while he registered. The wide reception area gave way to a lower level with long sofas dotted around, and further down she could just make out a bar.

'Ready?'

With a little nod, she smiled vaguely at the uniformed boy who was holding their bags. Seeing he had her attention, he swaggered toward the lifts. It was an act which in normal circumstances would have made Justine smile, only at the moment she felt too tired.

Their rooms were not only functional, but almost luxurious, the décor and furnishings of a much higher standard than their English counterparts. Kiel had the room adjoining hers, and both looked out over the rear of the hotel and terrace. Walking across to the window, she threw the shutters back. Wide steps led down to a sparkling pool with white wooden sun loungers lined up neatly on each side. Leaning her forehead tiredly against the window-frame, she gave a long sigh, then straightened reluctantly when a knock sounded.

'Hungry?' Kiel asked as he put his head round the door.

'Not really, more thirsty than anything, I think.' Holding the heavy weight of hair off her neck, she gave him a faint smile. She seemed to ache in every limb and the cast seemed suddenly to weigh a ton.

'Would you rather go straight to bed?' he asked gently. 'I can get a drink sent up to you, or you could join me in the bar; I can probably get a sandwich or something.'

'You could have a meal,' she argued half-heartedly. 'You don't have to wet-nurse me, you know.'

With a wry look that made her lips twitch, he held the door wide for her to pass through.

'What would you like?' he asked as they settled themselves on a padded bench seat in the bar.

'A large vodka,' then she grinned ruefully, 'only I'm not allowed. Doctor's orders. No alcohol, no stress, no undue exertion,' she intoned much as the doctor had done. 'I'll just have coffee, please. White. I seem to remember you have to stress the milk otherwise you automatically get it black. And will you please stop looking at me as though you think I'm going to pass out? It's totally out of character and beginning to worry me.'

Turning her earlier words back on her, he grinned. 'Overdoing it a bit, am I?'

'Yes!'

Laughing, he walked across to the bar.

Watching him, she gave a faint rueful smile. There was a vitality about him, a zest for living, a warmth that drew people. He didn't seem a bit bothered by the fact that he didn't speak the language, and she watched in amusement his efforts to be understood. It wasn't only herself who watched him either; most of the other people in the bar were too, not only the women, but then he was the most impressive person there. Not only exceptionally attractive, but his height and assurance, his slightly arrogant air, would no doubt always get him noticed. Not the sort of man one could overlook, and she guessed that whatever the occasion he would fit in with ease. If he wanted to, that was, she amended humorously. Those broad shoulders would probably look equally at home in a wet-suit or dinner-jacket, the long legs elegant in expensive trousers or jeans. When he laughed at something the barman said, she felt a funny little shiver go through her. His teeth gleamed whitely in his tanned face, and the shock of fair hair, which he still hadn't had cut, stood out with startling clarity against so many dark-haired people. He looked what he was: a wealthy, confident man with the knowledge that he would be accepted everywhere.

When he returned with her coffee and a lager for himself, she looked away, pretending an absorption in the other drinkers, and was rather unnerved when his powerful thigh touched against hers. Glancing at him, she gave a little snort of amusement when she saw from his face that he was offering deliberate provocation.

'Games, Kiel?'

With a faint smile, he shook his head. 'Tell me about when you were here before, all you remember, what you did, where you went.' Turning only his head, he gave her a devastating smile. His eyes were crinkled with amusement and she looked at him suspiciously.

'Are you by any chance flirting with me?'

'Mm,' he murmured on a thread of laughter.

'Why?'

'All pretty girls like to be flirted with,' he announced with unconscious arrogance.

'Rubbish!' she denied shortly. 'Anyway, I'm not pretty.'

'No-o, not in the accepted sense perhaps,' he agreed mockingly, 'but you have a certain... charm. A beautiful mouth, and the loveliest eyes I think I have ever seen. So tell me about before,' he continued without allowing her to comment. 'You never know, something might emerge.'

Yes, like a punch on the nose. Leaning back, her coffee-cup held between her palms, she forced her mind back nearly ten years. 'I was seventeen—God, what a lifetime ago that seems. David was being arbitrary, I do remember that, probably already regretting his quixotic behaviour. We took a taxi from the airport, much like today. I don't remember that it took very long, not hours or anything.' Lapsing into silence for a moment as she gazed back into the past, she continued thoughtfully, 'The villa had a little hedge round it; a wrought-iron gate with a latch that stuck. There was a kitchen, two bedrooms I think, a long hall with parquet flooring—and a cockroach,' she announced, sounding almost triumphant. She remembered that she wouldn't let David kill it, but made him capture it and put it outside.

'Oh, well, that should help,' he commented humorously. 'Go on, you're doing fine.'

'I don't remember things on a day-to-day basis,' she resumed slowly. 'It's all sort of jumbled together. We took the bus into Funchal, a battered old bus that only seemed to have two speeds, suicidal or stop.' Laughing, her face animated and almost beautiful, she added, 'Every time he needed to stop, the driver just slammed on his brakes so that all his passengers ended up in a heap on the floor... I remember the kapok trees in Funchal. I remember they made me laugh. I hadn't known kapok grew on trees, I'd always thought it was synthetic. David made some very disparaging remarks about my ignorance, I recall. What else? I remember the wicker sleds that slide down the cobbles into the town, only I never got to go on one,' she added faintly as a wave of dizziness washed over her. When her vision distorted rather alarmingly, she blinked rapidly and put up her hand to rub her fingers across her forehead in an effort to minimise the pain that seemed to be gradually building up.

'Headache?' he asked gently.

'Mm, it seems to have been a very long day.'

'Bed, then—we can continue tomorrow.' Draining the last of his drink, he got to his feet.

'But we only have a few days,' she protested worriedly.

'And if you knock yourself up you won't be any help at all,' he pointed out reasonably. 'Come on.'

Replacing her cup on the table, she stood and was more than grateful for his support when she swayed. 'Have you ever had concussion?' she asked inconsequentially.

'Mm, and numerous broken bones.'

'And I bet you coped wonderfully well, were a model patient, full of stamina and tolerance——'

'No,' he broke in, grinning, 'I was a royal pain in the neck. Impatient, irritable, not to say evil-tempered. That make you feel better?'

'No,' she denied as she summoned up a smile. 'But I will go quietly to my bed. Goodnight, Kiel.'

'Goodnight, Justine. Can you find your way all right?'

'Well, if I can't, I can always ask,' she retorted drily. 'I'm a big girl now.'

'Mm, so I perceive,' he mocked teasingly.

Shaking her head at him, she made her way upstairs. Leaning tiredly back against her bedroom door, she thought briefly over the day. She had been so sure that morning of her feelings for Kiel Lindstrom—and now she wasn't sure at all. Flirting with her, indeed. Walking across to the dressing-table, she stared at herself in the mirror. Did she have a nice mouth? With a self-mocking smile, she turned away. Don't be silly, Justine; flirting comes as easily as breathing to someone like that. True, but why bother with her? As far as he believed, she was the one who was trying to take David away from his sister. Too tired to try and work it out, she got ready for bed.

When she woke in the morning, she felt a lot better. Her head felt clear, and her arm seemed to have stopped throbbing, which was a relief. Cautiously sitting up, she smiled; the vertigo also seemed to have disappeared. Obviously she had been expecting too much of herself the day before. It vas, after all, her first full day out of hospital. Her awareness of Kiel had probably been all part and parcel of the concussion. Ever since the accident, she'd been coiled as tightly as a spring, but now, after a good night's sleep, she felt refreshed, relaxed. Reassured that she was nearly back to normal, and hadn't, as she had feared after her irrational behaviour, suffered a personality change, she went to wash.

Pulling on the tracksuit Kiel had bought her, she examined herself in the mirror. It rather suited her slim figure, she decided. The lavender shade gave her face some much-needed colour, made her eyes look brighter. Also, it fitted easily over her cast. Definitely a bonus point. Putting the hated sling back on, she walked across to the window. Throwing the shutters wide to the bright, sparkling morning, she stared out across the bay to the far headland. Everything looked freshly washed in the sunshine, which gilded the roofs of the villas and turned the blue waters of the bay to gold. It was like this all year round, she remembered reading—a temperate climate of between seventy and eighty degrees, although they did have violent storms from time to time. Fluffy white clouds seemed to linger over the hill-tops as though reluctant to pass on, and she closed her eyes, the better to enjoy the balmy breeze that stirred her long hair. If it hadn't been for David and the wretched plans, or Kiel's disturbing presence, she could have strolled down to the town, looked in the shops. And if it hadn't been for the damned plaster cast, she could have gone windsurfing. Already one or two sails dotted the bay.

'Up, I see,' a disgruntled voice observed from the doorway.

Swinging round in surprise, she stared at Kiel. He seemed to have suffered a reversal in spirit. He'd obviously washed and shaved, but the effort seemed to have exhausted him.

'No smart remarks, thank you, Justine,' he continued abrasively. 'Are you ready for breakfast?'

'Yes, I even feel quite hungry,' she murmured as she continued to stare at him. Perhaps he hadn't slept too well. Some people didn't in strange beds. Or maybe he was just one of those moody people. She hoped not, otherwise it was going to be an even more fraught few days than she had anticipated, but she was relieved to find that her awareness of him had evaporated.

Kiel ordered just coffee for himself when they were seated in the dining-room, and, with a gleam of humour in her lovely eyes, Justine ordered a full breakfast, and, when it was brought, tucked hungrily in.

When a small commotion broke out in the doorway, she looked up curiously. A man she vaguely remembered from the bar the night before had apparently stumbled into someone's table. He looked ten times worse than Kiel, and a possible reason for her companion's behaviour occurred to her. Glancing at the closed face opposite, the dark gold lashes that hid his eyes, she asked lightly, 'How long did you stay down in the bar last night?'

Looking up at her, his eyes blank and coldly green, he admitted reluctantly, 'Till four. But it wasn't in the bar.' Glancing sideways as the other man stumbled past them, he added grumpily, 'At least I can walk straight.'

'Only just,' she teased. 'Where did you go? And what on earth were you drinking?'

'God knows; some local brew down at the harbour with the fishermen. It seemed like a good idea at the time.'

About to remark that he hadn't seemed the sort of man to drink to excess, she wisely held her tongue, but nevertheless enjoyed the mental vision of Kiel stumbling back to the hotel, drunk as a skunk.

Pushing her empty plate to one side, she poured herself coffee and changed the subject. 'So what's on the agenda for today?'

'What? Oh, I got a map from the barman last night.' Leaning sideways, he produced a tightly folded map from his hip pocket. Moving the breakfast things aside, he spread it across the table. 'I also asked him if there was an English community, just on the off chance, but he said not many English come to Madeira. Do any of these names ring a bell?' he added, as he swept a large blunt-fingered hand across the map.

Leaning forward, she stared at the uneven coastline and the thinly spread names of the villages. 'It wouldn't be anywhere totally unpopulated,' she mumbled, in an effort to disguise the fact that nothing brought back a glimmer of memory, 'so that rules out quite vast stretches. I definitely remember that his villa was in a huddle with quite a few others. On a hill, I think... What was that for?' she exclaimed when he gave a snort of exasperation.

'The island is volcanic, Justine,' he pointed out impatiently.

'So?'

'So everything is on a hill or a damned mountain!'

'How do you know?' she demanded, a rather militant gleam in her eye. If he thought he could browbeat her, he had another think coming. Just because she'd been weak and malleable the day before...

'Because I asked the barman!'

'Oh, well, at least your marathon drink-in produced something other than a hangover,' she retorted sarcastically.

'Can we just get back to the map?' he asked wearily.

Pulling a little face, she returned her attention to the table.

'How long did it take on the bus?'

'I don't know. Not that long, I don't think, but it *was* ten years ago.'

'So you keep damned well telling me. I don't want an exact itinerary, for goodness' sake, just a rough estimate! A long time? Short? What?'

Blowing her breath out on a long explosion of air, she stared up at the ceiling as she tried to remember. 'Well, I don't think it was long... but then neither was it short! I simply don't know, Kiel. And it's no good looking like that; I told you before we came that it would be like looking for a needle in a haystack!'

'I'm well aware of what you told me, thank you— certainly I don't need chapter and verse all over again. Now, are you sure it was on the coast?'

'No. I'm not sure of anything,' she denied mutinously. All her pleasure in feeling better was rapidly evaporating; the man was a positive Jekyll and Hyde.

Striving manfully to sound reasonable, and—in Justine's opinion—failing miserably, he instructed,

'All right, we'll take the bus into Funchal, see what that produces.'

'Can't we hire a car?'

'No, we can't. We have to reproduce your journey, and we can hardly do that in a car. Are you ready?'

'I suppose so.' Getting to her feet, she put her bag back on her shoulder, then had to wait for him to refold the map. 'Do you know where the bus goes from?'

'No, Justine, I do not know where the bus goes from, I will ask at the desk.'

With a little grimace at his rapidly retreating back, unaware that their behaviour was causing untold amusement to the other people in the dining-room, she followed him. '"Whither thou goest",' she muttered sarcastically, then swung round startled when she heard a smothered laugh.

'That's it, love, start as you mean to go on.'

'Yes,' she agreed weakly, then chuckled, 'Chance would be a fine thing.'

The bus was every bit as bad as she remembered. It might even have been the same one; certainly the driver might. Unless they were all trained by the same maniac instructor... and the thought of such a driving-school made her lips twitch.

'What do you find so damned funny?'

'Nothing,' she denied on a long sigh. 'Just thoughts.' Certainly he was in no mood to appreciate any humour in the situation.

Taking her seat, she watched as he lowered himself beside her. One strong-muscled forearm was inches from her own as he clasped the seat in front, and the gold Rolex round his wrist seemed to emphasise the blond hairs, bleached lighter by the sun and salt—from his sailing, she supposed absently. The dark green shirt he was wearing, the sleeves rolled casually back, emphasised the colour of his eyes. Not that she thought it was intentional on his part; to date she hadn't found him in the least conceited. He probably didn't care what people thought; he didn't even seem to notice the stares he got. Perhaps it was just his height that made him so commanding. She barely reached his shoulder, and yet, at five feet six, she wasn't exactly short. Yes, she finally decided, this odd awareness she kept experiencing was probably only because of his height. Feeling slightly better for having explained it satisfactorily to herself, she transferred her gaze to the window.

'Anything?' he suddenly asked.

With a guilty start, she brought her attention back to the reason for the bus journey. 'No, not yet,' she denied hastily. Concentrating on the view, and finding nothing even remotely familiar, she shook her head in added denial, and yet surely if she had been down this hairpin gorge they were now descending—far too fast in her opinion—she would have remembered it? And then, just for a moment, she did. The wreck of a yellow Volkswagen was lying at the bottom and she had a definite memory of having seen it before. Screwing her eyes up in concentration, she was unaware that Kiel was watching her intently, almost willing her to remember—but the moment was lost as the bus jolted to a sudden stop. Peering ahead, as was everyone else, amid the excited conversation that suddenly broke out, she stood as Kiel got up to look.

'We're going to have to back up,' he explained. 'The road's not wide enough for the van in front to get past.' Losing interest, he resumed his seat, and when Justine didn't immediately do so he tugged her down to sit beside him. 'Well?' he demanded impatiently. 'So what did you remember?'

'What? Oh, nothing very much.' Giving him her full attention, she explained, 'I just thought that I must have been along this road before, because I remember the yellow Volkswagen down there.' Pointing to show what she meant, she tutted irritably when he leaned against her to peer from the window.

'And that's it?' he asked in astonishment.

'Well, I'm very sorry! I'm doing my best!' Very aware of the disgruntled glance he gave her, and, unfortunately, the tang of his aftershave, she pushed him back into his own seat. She'd also been rather too aware of the warmth of his muscled arm pressing against her own. So much for getting over her awareness of him, she thought drearily. When he slanted her an odd glance that she was unable to interpret, she hastily returned her gaze to the window and was inordinately thankful when the bus ground into motion once more.

Nothing else on the hour-long journey into the capital even remotely tugged at her memory, and she climbed down beside him at the terminal feeling thoroughly despondent.

'I wonder what the odds are of David being here at the same time as ourselves?' she mused aloud as she gazed along the road towards the harbour.

'Remote,' he said shortly.

'Yeah. So now what?' she asked on a long sigh.

When he didn't answer, she turned her head to look at him. He was staring round him with a frown on his face, hands jammed into his pockets, legs astride.

'Don't you remember anything at all?'

'No,' she denied despondently. Putting her hand up to control her unruly hair that was blowing all over the place, she gazed round her, much as Kiel was doing. 'Shall we walk round for a bit? You never know, something might click.'

Without answering, he began to stride up towards the town, and Justine hastened after him. Nothing seemed familiar to her at all. Seeing a bank, she remembered her need to change some money. 'Can we stop for a minute? I need to go in the bank.'

'If you must.' Giving her a look of discouragement, he leaned against the bank wall.

Pulling her mouth down at his sulky behaviour, she asked curiously, 'Don't you need to change some?'

'No, I already changed some at the hotel. How else would I pay for the bus tickets?'

'You could have changed some in England—and I'd be enormously grateful if you'd stop taking your bad temper out on me.'

'I'm not in a temper,' he denied crossly.

No, no, all sweetness and light, she grumbled to herself as she went into the welcome coolness of the bank. Changing fifty pounds, which she assumed should be ample, she put the money and her passport back into her bag. Presumably Kiel was paying the hotel bill, and she certainly didn't see why she should spend a lot of her own money when it was he who'd insisted she come.

As soon as she joined him, he instructed, 'You'd better get yourself some sunglasses. This sun won't do your head any good.'

Irritated for not having thought of it herself, she walked moodily into the pharmacy next door. Even the most obvious things seemed to escape her. Buying the first pair of sunglasses that fitted, she also purchased a hairband, which the shop assistant kindly used to put her hair up into a pony-tail. When she emerged, Kiel viewed the changed hairstyle as though he hated it.

'Where now?'

'How should I know? You're the expert.'

Clenching her jaw on a rude retort, she turned to walk up the hill.

'That doesn't lead anywhere,' he told her squashingly.

'How do you know? You said you hadn't been to Madeira before.'

'I haven't. I bought a map while you were in the bank, and, as you were such a long time, I had ample opportunity to study it.'

Glaring at him, she turned and stalked off. Miserable sod. Disagreeable, miserable so and so. Did he think she found it easy? Think she was doing it on purpose just to thwart him? Her eyes unexpectedly blurring with tears, she sniffed and brushed them impatiently away.

'Look,' he began. He grabbed her arm and hauled her round to face him, then a comical expression of dismay crossed his face. 'Oh, God, you're not going to cry, are you?' he asked wearily. 'I can't bear women who cry. Do you want to rest?'

'No,' she denied stonily. Shrugging her arm away, she found a tissue in her bag and gave her nose a good blow. Ignoring his muttered imprecation, she began walking towards the centre of the town.

As they walked rather aimlessly round, both were silent. His thoughts, judging by his expression, were bordering on murderous, and she sighed. She'd told him it would be no good.

When they entered the square, and Justine saw the kapok trees, she came to a halt, her irritation with him forgotten. Staring up at the tall trees, she murmured softly, 'There's a shoe shop near here, Charles Shoes—that way,' she suddenly exclaimed. Pointing left, her eyes blank, she retraced the route she saw in her mind. 'There,' she said triumphantly. 'And down here,' she added, giving his arm an impatient tug, 'there's an open-air café that's shaded by an enormous tree. Yes!' she exclaimed in satisfaction as she saw the tables and chairs that spilled out across the pavement. 'There's a new indoor shopping centre—or it was new ten years ago,' she qualified, 'and a municipal garden; David took me there for a rest, only the cobbles were so uneven that David twisted his ankle.' Turning to look up at him, she smiled warmly, only to find that he was looking at her very oddly. She got the impression that he wasn't seeing her at all, but some other vision that didn't quite please him. 'Kiel?' she queried softly.

'Mm?' As his eyes came back into focus, he smiled. 'Clever girl. Then what did you do? Have a drink?'

Still searching his face, a frown in her eyes, she nodded.

'OK, then we'll do the same.' His earlier temper might never have been as he led her towards a vacant table. He smiled at the waitress, he smiled at her, and Justine stared at him in astonishment.

'What's wrong?' he queried with such an innocent expression that she could have hit him.

'Wrong? What could be wrong?' she asked with soft sarcasm. 'Everything's just hunky-dory.'

'Oh, good. What will you have, coffee?'

'No, a cold drink, please.'

The waitress obviously understood English, because she smiled and jotted it down on her pad. Kiel ordered coffee for himself—presumably to cure the hangover he probably still had.

The service was very fast, and within a few minutes the waitress was back with their order. With a quiet thank-you for the young girl, she leaned back, and allowed her eyes to roam across the little square. A mangy dog was lying in the middle of the road, sunning himself. Totally disregarded by the people bustling about, mostly students, she saw. She gave a faint smile. Nice to be a dog. Nice to be a student, yet the merged sound of their voices was a soothing babble, and Justine gradually relaxed. What had Kiel been thinking about when he'd stared at her so oddly? she wondered. Turning her head, she stared at him. He too was leaning back, staring idly round him, and the sun shining through the leaves of the tree above them dappled his face and added yet another dimension to his attractiveness. As in the hotel, people were giving him covert glances, of which he seemed totally unaware. Despite the casual clothes, and the relaxed air, there was still an aura of wealth and power about him. A remoteness that was intriguing. As if aware of her glance, he turned towards her, and raised his eyebrows in query.

With a little shake of her head, she picked up her glass.

'We ought to make a move,' he prompted. 'What did you do before?'

'Walked back to the bus depot,' she answered lazily. She felt no desire to move at all, would have been quite happy to sit in the little café all day watching the world go by. Watching Kiel, try to understand him. Only of course she couldn't. Pointing to the little alley that ran from the square towards the harbour, she added reluctantly, 'Down that way.'

Putting a handful of change on the table to pay for their drinks, he finished his coffee. 'Ready?'

Nodding, she got to her feet and led the way to the alley. Kiel seemed to have withdrawn again, and, as they walked, was apparently absorbed by the activity down by the port. Certainly he kept his eyes trained in that direction, his face moody. Having no idea what had made him grumpy this time, she stayed silent as she brooded on the very odd relationship they seemed to have developed. One moment friendly, the next distant.

When they arrived at the bus depot, she stood awkwardly, waiting for him to make a decision. She felt tired now, and slightly light-headed, only after his previous behaviour she was damned if she was going to complain.

'What now?' she asked quietly.

'We go on another bus ride. Come here,' he added peremptorily.

Come here, go there, do this, do that. With an inward sigh, she joined him in front of the timetable that also helpfully gave a map of the route the bus took. 'Camacha,' she said with absolute conviction. David had sat on the little bench complaining about his ankle, and her mood that day hadn't been any happier than it was today. Was it her? she wondered suddenly, an arrested expression on her face. Was her behaviour responsible for other people being difficult?

'Justine!' Kiel snapped impatiently.

'What?' Reluctantly returning her attention to him, she blinked. 'Sorry, what did you say?'

'I said, are you sure?'

'Yes. I definitely remember David saying to look for a number seventy-seven.'

'Why couldn't he look for it?'

'Because he'd hurt his foot!' she snapped impatiently. Striving to hold on to her own temper, which was in danger of erupting at the very peremptory tone he was using, she glared at the map as she tried to find one name, one village, that seemed familiar.

'Some gentleman,' he denigrated.

'You're a fine one to talk,' she muttered rebelliously. To date his behaviour had been ten times worse than David's. 'Was it the action of a gentleman to drag me from my sick-bed? Was it gentlemanly to drag me all round Funchal?'

'Me drag you? Me?' he exclaimed in astonishment.

'All right, all right, me,' she agreed placatingly. She felt much too tired to embark on yet another pointless argument.

'Very well, we'll try a number seventy-seven,' he informed her arrogantly, 'and then walk wherever your blotchy memory takes us.'

'That's not fair, Kiel. I thought I'd done quite well, considering.'

'True, in Funchal, which is not exactly where we want you to remember anything. Charles Shoes and cafés do not advance our cause at all!'

'Don't be so unkind! It's not my fault that my memory only remembers incidentals.' Hurt by his unnecessarily scathing tone, she added crossly, 'Perhaps if you were a bit more considerate instead of snapping at me every five minutes, I'd be a bit more inclined to help!'

'If that means that you are being deliberately obstructive,' he gritted, 'I think I might hit you!'

'And if I believed that, I'd be straight back to the airport and home!' she yelled furiously. Turning away, she marched blindly along the row of buses until she came to a number seventy-seven. My God, the man was schizophrenic! Climbing on board, not caring if it was going anywhere or not, she huddled furiously on the back seat. How dared he speak to her like that? She was doing him a favour, for goodness' sake!

Ignoring the curious glances from people passing by outside, she kept her face averted as she felt the bus dip and Kiel climbed on board. She was damned if she was going to help him any more. Let him find David by himself! He was the most arrogant, inconsistent, moody...

'You're on the wrong bus, Justine,' he said mildly. His temper having subsided as quickly as it had erupted, he added, 'This one isn't going anywhere for another hour. It's the one alongside.'

'I don't care,' she denied mutinously. 'I don't care if it *never* goes anywhere. My head aches, my arm aches, my feet ache... And this damned sling is rubbing my neck sore!'

With a muffled snort of laughter, he folded his arms and leaned against the seat in front of her. 'I'm sorry I shouted,' he apologised softly. 'Come on.' Bending down, he took her gently by the arm to pull her upright. 'Look at me,' he instructed quietly when she kept her eyes riveted on the top button of his shirt.

Glancing reluctantly up, her mouth tight, her stormy eyes hidden behind the glasses, she refused to answer, then glared defiantly at him when he gave a rueful smile.

'I don't find it any easier than you do, Justine. So come on, don't give up on me now.'

Twitching her shoulder, which wasn't quite a shrug, she pushed past him and walked with marvellous sedateness round to the other bus. Climbing on board, she took a seat next to an elderly lady holding a live chicken. Kiel sat behind her, and, leaning forward, a thread of laughter in his voice, he whispered, 'You're making a big mistake.'

Not deigning to answer, she stared rigidly ahead.

'Honest,' he continued wickedly. 'If you've never sat next to a chicken before, you'll regret it before the journey's half over, believe me.'

'How do you know?' she demanded crossly. 'When have you ever sat next to a chicken?'

'In Greece, and it is not an experience I wish to repeat. Come on, stop sulking, come and sit here.'

With a disdainful little snort, she got up and plumped down beside him. The man was impossible. No sooner had she started liking him than he was horrible, and then when she decided she hated him he tried to make her smile. Well, she wasn't going to.

Camacha turned out to be very small. An art and craft shop that was shut; a pharmacy that was also closed; and none of it looked in any way familiar. Not that she told him that, merely retained a thoughtful silence as she accompanied him to the look-out point, named unpronounceably Aussichtspunkt Miradouro, which was a total disappointment because it was above the cloud formation and all they could see once they had climbed up was a scene that resembled nothing more inspiring than damp cotton wool that stretched as far as the eye could see. Beginning to feel decidedly unwell, she wasn't sorry when they made their way back down to the village. None of the villas dotted around bore any resemblance to the one in her mind—and yet she was so sure she remembered David saying Camacha.

'We'll have something to eat,' Kiel decided. 'That will make you feel better. Then we'll have another look round.'

Too tired to argue, she collapsed limply at a small garden table beside a restaurant in one of the little side-streets. He could have another look round if he wanted. She was too tired to do anything. It would take Superman to keep up with him. Didn't he ever relax? Keep still? Didn't he have any quiet moments? Watch the sun rise? Set? Staring at him, at the energy that seemed to pulsate from within him, even while he sat, she sighed.

CHAPTER FOUR

REFRESHED by the meal, which consisted of *bacalhau à Brás,* dried cod fried with onions and potatoes, then cooked with beaten egg—or so the phrase book said that Kiel had acquired from somewhere, presumably when she bought her sunglasses—Justine settled for fruit juice, Kiel for coffee, and they sat for a while, just relaxing. Or she did. Kiel looked as though he'd retreated to some dark and distant place. She hoped he wasn't going to sulk for the rest of the afternoon. Staring at a clump of bird of paradise flowers, which seemed to grow everywhere, she jumped when he spoke.

'Not talking to me? Not that I can blame you...'

Swinging round to stare at him in astonishment, she was unable for a moment to think what to say.

Slanting her a wry glance, he continued with unexpected candour, 'I'm sorry, Justine, I've been a royal pain, haven't I?'

'Yes,' she agreed firmly.

With one of his abrupt laughs, he took her hand and held it firmly between his strong fingers. His eyes on hers, a rueful smile in their depths, he explained simply, 'It's guilt.'

'Guilt?'

'Mm, for dragging you round when you're clearly unwell. I've also been worried about the future of the yard,' he added quietly. 'Without this order—which, even if I find David and the plans, isn't definite— they are going to find it very hard to get out of the red.'

Watching him curiously, she asked something that had been puzzling her, 'Why are you going to all this trouble for a man you don't even like very much?'

'You mean David?' When she nodded, he gave a wry smile. 'Purely selfish reasons—well, no,' he corrected, 'that's not entirely true, although if I can get David settled it will keep Katia off my back! And even without the plans, I would probably have come. He needs to be brought to a sense of his own responsibilities. Katia loves him, and I won't see her hurt any more. But mostly it's for John. He and I are old friends. He's also a brilliant designer. He's had a lot of bad luck lately, and I'd like to see that change. His confidence is pretty rocky at the moment, and if he could get this order, not only will it help save Naughton's, but it will give him a much-needed boost. It's a really *good* design, and it would be the greatest pity if he lost out through no fault of his own.'

'Do you know how many other tenders are likely to be submitted?' she asked sympathetically.

'No, but at least four others I should think. A lot of the yards are in the same position as Naughton's. It's a very fickle market, marine design; one season everyone wants yachts, for racing, pleasure. The next it's speedboats...'

'I see. And is this for a yacht?'

'Yes. There's been some success with this type, initially raced at Cowes last year, and it's hoped it will do well this year. Although, strictly speaking, even if they get the order, it's doubtful if it will be ready in time for this season, but once the order is secure it could lead to others. Yachtsmen tend to follow each other, especially if there has been a success. Much like racing cars, I suppose.'

'You race, don't you? Yachts, I mean; I seem to remember David saying you were in the Fastnet one year.'

'Mm.' Then, with a rueful smile, he admitted, 'We came ninth. I don't do so much now, don't have the time; my life seems permanently divided between my own yard in Norway and Naughton's.'

'Because David isn't very good or useful there?'

'Partly,' he admitted, 'although, as I said, it's a fickle business; there's always the thought that next year will end it, or the season after that. At the moment, yachting is popular, clubs springing up on available waterways...'

'But by next year it could be horse riding, or water-skiing?' she queried lightly, and when he smiled she continued, 'It's a similar situation in the travel business. Deals, cheap package tours to tempt the holidaymaker. The bucket shops don't help, of course, with their reduced fare deals. Get a wet summer and bookings go up. Get a good one and people decide to stay home. Quite a few travel companies have merged, or been taken over altogether.'

'But not yours,' he commented with another faint smile. 'Golf holidays are popular, I take it?'

'At the moment, yes.'

'Well, let's hope it stays that way,' he encouraged absently, 'but for now I think we had best get on with our quest.'

When he got to his feet, she remained sitting for a moment, staring up at him. 'I am trying, Kiel,' she told him earnestly, 'but I honestly don't remember.'

'I know. It's just so damnably frustrating.'

'And I'm not having an affair with David,' she added quietly. 'I told you the truth.'

For a moment, he didn't speak, just continued to gaze down at her, his eyes almost empty, then with a little nod, as if to confirm it to himself, he said, 'All right, I'll accept that.'

'Thank you.' With a little sigh of relief, she got to her feet. Feeling a great deal better, as though a weight had been lifted, she gave him a warm smile. Although why his opinion should matter she had no idea. It didn't normally bother her what people might think, only, for some odd reason, she wanted this man's approbation. Hastily pushing her thoughts aside, she said briskly, 'Right, let's go.

Somewhere on this island is my wayward cousin. It's a pity neither of us speak the language; it would be easier to make enquiries.'

'Just what I was thinking. However, with my trusty phrase book, I will try and find out from mine host whether he knows of an Englishman living round here. Knowing David, I doubt he does his own cooking, which means he uses restaurants.'

'Logical,' she approved, then wondered at the laugh he gave. Perhaps because other people's approval didn't come high on his list of priorities.

While he went to make enquiries, she absently pondered his complex personality, and in particular his ability to make her like him, almost against her will. Thinking back over past relationships, she shook her head in bewilderment. No man she had been out with had ever spoken to her as Kiel did, and yet she liked him the more for it. Crazy. He made her angry, he exasperated her, and he made her laugh. And yet, without David and his sister, tying them to a relationship, would he have even looked at her? No. She was no beauty to attract someone like Kiel. Wasn't startlingly witty; didn't have a terrific figure. Apart from her eyes, she was ordinary, or so she considered. It wasn't an opinion shared by others. Her face had a gentle beauty, a warmth. Her smile was genuine and delightful, and her courage and determination to set up her own business without help or encouragement had won her a great deal of admiration.

When Kiel returned, looking smugly self-satisfied, she looked at him hopefully. 'You've found something out?'

'Mm. He lives round here somewhere. At least the restaurant owner says there's an Englishman comes in for meals sometimes. Pity neither of us thought to bring a photograph. Still, it's a start. Ready?'

'Yes, of course. What do you want to do? Wander round in the hope we might see him?' It didn't seem very likely, and her voice reflected her uncertainty. No one had that sort of luck.

'For the lack of any brilliant alternatives, yes. If you're not too tired?'

'You said that as though daring me not to be,' she exclaimed on a laugh. 'But no, I feel fine now. Maybe we could try the restaurants tonight.'

'We'll see how you feel after I've dragged you up a few hills. It will be a long day for you,' he warned.

'Concerned for my health?' she teased.

'No, that you might slow me down,' he corrected drily.

Which was probably the exact truth, she reflected wryly, and then was rather amazed to find that she was disappointed that her usefulness might be at an end. She hadn't wanted to come, considered he had blackmailed her into it, so she should be pleased that he might no longer need her. Only she wasn't. How perverse.

On his own, he would have gone striding around, up and down the steep hills without discomfort, but strangely he didn't seem to find it irksome to match his pace to hers. He even tucked her hand into his arm, and they walked almost companionably round with Kiel treating her with a fatherly concern that tickled her. In truth she was quite enjoying it. It had been a long time since anyone had shown her such consideration; not that she expected it to last, she thought humorously. It would take only one word said in the wrong place, or in the wrong tone, and back he would be to his usual impossible self.

'You're very quiet,' he commented quietly. 'Tired?'

'No,' she denied, 'I was just thinking.'

'About what?'

'Oh, nothing in particular, just letting my mind wander.'

'That doesn't sound a very profitable exercise,' he teased lightly.

'No,' she agreed with a faint smile. Did he never indulge in idle daydreams? she wondered. It certainly didn't sound like it, and, as they walked, she began to speculate about him. What was he like to sail under? Was he a harsh taskmaster? Exacting? Did he set impossible standards? Then she denied the thought. He would be fair, she decided, as long as people were honest about their abilities. Was that the trouble with David? That he would never admit to his inadequacies? Muddling along, defiant in the face of his limitations?

Gradually, so that she was hardly aware of it at first, she began to feel a sense of familiarity. There was nothing definite, nothing she could put her finger on, but she had the distinct feeling that she had walked these streets before, seen these same views. The little white church with the tall spire; the glimpse of blue sea through the trees; the tiny gardens with the riot of flowers that everyone so loved; the banana trees, and she unconsciously slowed her steps. 'It is here,' she murmured. 'I'm sure of it.' Raising her eyes to his, she added wryly, 'Only I'm not exactly sure where.'

'All right, perhaps if we walk up a bit higher,' he suggested, 'and look down on the town, you might recognise something, be able to pinpoint it.'

'Perhaps.' Taking the hand he held out, she allowed him to help her up the steep hill. She liked the feel of his warm, strong fingers curled round her own, she discovered, and was forced to hastily banish thoughts that intruded of further intimacies with this vital man. Ever since the accident, her life had seemed out of control, directed by both David and Kiel. Both men so different, yet equally capable of confusing her. If she could at least find David, or his villa, it would be something positive, a sort of anchor for her to latch on to. She still had no memory of crashing the car, taking David to the airport, and it worried her. Part of her life was missing, two vital days, days in which she might have done anything. Her own behaviour, too, was hardly something to be proud of. She'd been crotchety, irrational, in fact totally unlike her normal self, and she prayed that it was only because of the concussion. If it wasn't, she was in for an uncomfortable time of it.

When they reached a little track that curved between the prow of the hill and a banana plantation, Justine thankfully sat on the bank behind her. Only a mountain goat could go any higher—or Kiel, she admitted with a little grin as he began pulling himself up on the tussocky grass until he found a foothold. He stood like the proud Viking she had once likened him to, one hand shading his eyes as he stared down towards the town—and then gave an enormous yell that had Justine leaping to her feet in alarm.

'What?' she exclaimed as he bounded past her and plunged into the undergrowth. 'Kiel! You can't just wade though someone's plantation!'

'Why not?' he threw over his shoulder, then had of necessity to slow down. The trees didn't grow tidily in rows and he had to thread his way impatiently between them.

'Well, if you don't know why at your age,' she yelled in exasperation, 'it's a bit late for me to teach you your manners!'

'I'm not going to damage it, for goodness' sake! David's down there!'

'Where?' But she was talking to herself, because Kiel had already disappeared from sight. She could hear him crashing about, and, her expression highly indicative of her thoughts, she looked guiltily around before plunging after him.

Although the banana palms weren't very high, only seven feet or so, they were wide, with large leaves, which when dried were used for roofing the local houses, or for weaving baskets or fencing, and they impeded her awkward progress. With only one arm for balance, she gained unwilling momentum on the sloping ground, and when her feet slipped from under her on the squelchy leaf mould she made an unlooked for jarring descent on her bottom. Cursing banana plantations in general, and Kiel in particular, she put out her hand to pull herself up, then screamed in fright when her fingers touched something furry. She imagined it to be a tarantula at the very least; her fear propelled her up and downwards with a speed that was her further undoing. Tripping, she fell headlong, and Kiel, who had turned back on hearing her scream, took the full brunt of her hurtling body, which sent them both backwards in a tangle of limbs and foliage.

'Of all the damned, silly, stupid... Are you insane? You could have killed us both!'

With the breath knocked out of her, she lay still for a few moments, too stunned to think, let alone answer him, and when she did manage to open her eyes she found herself staring, from very close quarters, into Kiel's furious face. She also, belatedly, became aware that her body was resting almost intimately against his solid frame. One leg was trapped between his strong thighs, and she could feel every muscle and sinew through her thin clothing. With a long shudder that she was unable to contain, she blushed furiously.

His own voice none too steady, he demanded, 'What in God's name happened?'

None too sure if it was his proximity or the aftermath of the fall that made her feel so unsteady, she whispered, 'Spider.'

'Spider? Spider?'

'Yes! Spider! You don't need to echo it with such disbelief. I don't like spiders! And will you please let me get up?'

With an exasperated grunt, he disentangled himself, and struggled upright. Extending a hand, he hauled her unceremoniously to her feet. Taking in the state of her, he exploded, 'I told you to stay at the top!'

'You did not!' Her voice a curious mixture of anger and embarrassment, she added furiously, 'You didn't say anything at all, just went crashing into the plantation!' Which wasn't strictly true—however, she wasn't about to bring up incidentals at that point, she still felt thoroughly shaken, but not, she thought, by the fall. The imagined spider was now completely forgotten. She also found that she was unable to look at him, and made a great production of brushing herself down.

'Well, I hardly expected you to follow suit! Honestly, Justine, I sometimes wonder if you have a brain!'

His voice didn't sound totally convincing either, and tension shimmered between them, charging the air.

'Oh, charming!' Desperately trying to hide her confused feelings behind a mask of anger, she added, 'Thank you very much! I risk life and limb...'

'For absolutely no reason that I can think of,' he bit out furiously.

'No! Neither can I now! Why not put it down to feminine perversity? Or an insane desire to plunge myself into the undergrowth!' Taking a deep, shaky breath, she wiped her muddy palm down her thigh. 'Did you find him?' she managed more calmly.

'How could I find him?' he demanded incredulously. 'When you screamed, I naturally turned back.'

'Oh, naturally, your concern for my health is overwhelming. It didn't seem to bother you much when you dragged me down to Funchal!'

'Oh, don't start that again,' he said wearily.

'Oh, go and find David.' Hobbling past him, she perched on a boulder at the side of the road. 'I'm all right,' she insisted.

'Yes, you damned well look it! You've got a scratch on your cheek! You're covered in mud——'

'I'm all right!' she repeated fretfully. Wiping her hand across her cheek, which came away sticky with blood, she gave a long, heartfelt sigh. What an idiot. 'You go and find David, I'll just sit here for a bit...'

When he didn't immediately move, she peeped at him sideways, and felt her own lips twitch in response to the quiver in his.

'You are the most...' he began softly, but he was quite unable to keep his face straight, and suddenly they were both laughing helplessly.

'I'm sorry,' she gasped. 'I must have sounded like a fishwife.'

'Mm.' With a gentle hand he tucked a stray strand of hair behind her ear. 'Look a bit like one, too,' he added as he examined her dirty face. 'You've twisted your ankle...'

'I only wrenched it a bit when I fell,' she deprecated softly.

'And your arm...'

'My arm is fine.' At least she hoped it was. It didn't seem to ache or anything. Wriggling her fingers experimentally, she was relieved to find that everything seemed to work. 'I'm all right; go on, go and find David.'

With a last look at her and a rueful shake of his head, he swung away, and began to run lightly down the road. As soon as he was out of sight, she examined herself more closely. Her hand was filthy, as was the lavender suit that she had been so pleased with that morning. The sling looked as though it had been used as a cleaning rag; and the plaster looked as though it had been on for months instead of only days. Examining it for cracks, or other damage, and finding none, she pulled up one trouser leg to examine her sore ankle, and was disgusted to find that it looked no different from usual. No interesting swelling, no redness. Wrenching the trouser leg back down, she slid to the ground and leaned back against the boulder. Not very clever, Justine. No, but a smile still lurked in her eyes in memory of their laughter. She could also still almost feel the warmth and strength of him, the imprint of his body on hers, and she gave a little shiver. It might be best not to remember that bit—or the warmth in his green eyes as he had stared down at her.

Suddenly feeling tired, and a little bit depressed, she rested her head on her updrawn knees and so didn't see Kiel returning. The first she knew of his presence was his quiet, concerned voice from beside her.

'Are you all right?'

Raising her head with a start, she accepted the sunglasses he was holding out. 'Yes, I'm fine. Did you find him?'

'No. Oh, well,' he added philosophically, 'at least we know he's here somewhere. Come on, I'll take you back to the hotel.'

Opening her mouth to argue, she changed her mind; she was hardly in any fit state to continue the search.

'Very wise,' he said drily.

'Yes, I thought you might think so,' she retorted with a smile that wasn't nearly as light as she was pretending. 'Like your women obedient, don't you?'

'My women?' he queried softly. 'Is that what you are?'

Staring at him in astonishment, which quickly turned to confusion when he gave her a slow smile, she felt herself blush. Deciding rather frantically that it would be best not to answer; didn't know how to answer in fact, because it was a thought that brought no displeasure at all. On the contrary, the mere thought of being his woman, and all that would entail, made her insides curl. Getting hastily to her feet, she agitatedly brushed herself down. How could she be so stupid as to even consider it? His question, if question it was, had been purely rhetorical, certainly not to be taken as an invitation. Anyway, she didn't want that, not really. Emotional involvement left you vulnerable, open to hurt, as she of all people should know only too well. She had laid herself wide open to Aunt Margaret's snubs when she was a child needing warmth and affection, and had vowed then to be very, very careful who she gave her heart to. Up until now, it had been a vow very easy to keep. Her body might sometimes want comfort, warmth, but she had never met anyone that gave her the least inclination to throw her cap over the windmill. Until now? an insidious voice asked silently.

Giving him a wary glance, she forced a smile when he grinned.

'Do you have any idea, I wonder, how appealing you look at this precise moment?' he asked humorously. 'With a long scratch decorating one cheek, your hair an untidy tangle, your eyes a startling contrast to your dirty face, you look like a grubby, and endearing, urchin. Come on,' he encouraged, holding one hand out to her, 'I'd best try and smuggle you into the hotel by the back door.'

With a rather defeated attempt at light-heartedness, she asked huskily, 'That bad, huh?'

''Fraid so; we don't want people to think I've been beating you up.'

'We don't?' she teased. But beneath her light tone was a tension she didn't know how to dispel. There had been a warmth in his eyes that hadn't been there before, a note in his voice that she couldn't analyse.

'No, Justine, we don't,' he said firmly, but with just the faintest twitch to his lips, 'tempting as the idea may be for you.'

Walking slowly back into the town, he threw one arm companionably round her shoulders, and the warm, heavy weight only added to her confusion. 'What will we do about David?' she asked quickly. 'Come back later?'

'I will come back later,' he said firmly, 'alone.'

'Oh, but——'

'No buts, Justine—as you pointed out, I have done quite enough dragging you around today.'

'I didn't say that,' she protested faintly, 'I only said—— '

'I know what you only said. What a girl you are for arguing.'

'Only with you,' she sighed. Normally she had a very equable temper. It was only with Kiel that she seemed to flare up at the slightest provocation.

'Well, whatever the reasons, you are going to rest this evening. If I don't find him, there's still tomorrow.'

As he had promised, he smuggled her in the back way. The taxi driver dropped them by the rear entrance to the pool, and fortunately the glass-walled boutiques just inside the hotel were not yet open, so there was no one to see her scruffy state. She was also surprised to find that it was not yet five. The day seemed to have lasted a lot longer.

'Have a hot bath, soak some of those bruises out, then rest,' he admonished as he opened her door for her. 'I'm going to shower and change, and, if you're good, when I come back from searching for David I'll take you out for a meal and a drink.'

'Oh, what an inducement,' she replied sweetly, then yelped when he smacked her rear and pushed her into her room.

'If you need anything, bang on the wall,' he called as he disappeared into his own room.

Anything? she asked silently. I don't somehow think you'd be prepared to give what I think I'm beginning to need, then came to a shocked halt as she caught sight of herself in the mirror. 'Good grief!'

she exclaimed aloud. Bending forward, she peered intently at her reflection as though she couldn't believe she looked so awful. It was a wonder he hadn't refused to be seen with her! Wrenching off her hairband, she walked into the bathroom to run her bath.

Stripping off and dropping her clothes on the floor, she removed the mud-stained sling and put it in the basin to soak. Awkwardly cleansing and moisturising her face, she climbed carefully into the bath. It was so difficult doing everything one-handed; she'd be glad when the wretched plaster came off. Only another five weeks. Some comfort that was. Reaching for the shampoo, she jammed the bottle between the plaster cast and her body, and tried, unsuccessfully, to get the cap off. She tried using the flannel to gain purchase on the slippery bottle; the towel; even her teeth, and still the damned cap wouldn't budge. Taking a deep breath to contain the temper and frustration she could feel bubbling up, she tried again, then hurled the plastic bottle against the wall in fury and exasperation. Feeling enormously better for her childish action, she lay back. What idiot had put the top on so tight it would take Superman to get it off? Seeing as she lived alone and no one else ever used her shampoo, the question was rhetorical.

'What?' Kiel demanded as he crashed in and skidded to a comical halt on the tiled floor.

With a screech of alarm, Justine hastily slid under the water, nearly immersing the plaster cast in her agitation. 'What the hell are you doing in here? Get out!'

'You banged on the wall!'

'I did not!'

'Yes, you did! I heard a damned great crash!'

'Oh. Well, I wasn't knocking,' she said lamely, 'so you can go away again.'

'What was it?' he demanded as he advanced more cautiously across the room.

Feeling extremely stupid, she muttered, 'Nothing.'

'Nothing?' he queried lightly, a light of unholy amusement dancing in his eyes.

'All right! I threw the shampoo bottle at the wall! Happy now?'

'Oh, delirious—do that sort of thing often, do you?'

'No, I do not! And I wish you'd go away!'

Giving her a rather wolfish grin, he walked leisurely across to retrieve the shampoo bottle, and she noticed for the first time that his hair was still damp from his shower, and that he had changed into beige twill trousers and a brown and cream striped shirt that hung loosely outside as though he had just put it on when he heard the crash. Returning, he held the bottle in one large hand, and, his eyes fixed on hers, he twisted off the cap.

'Thank you,' she gritted.

'My pleasure,' he taunted softly as he handed it to her with a mocking flourish.

Averting her eyes from the expanse of bronzed chest, she took the bottle from him. 'I expect the cap loosened when it hit the wall,' she said peevishly.

'Yes,' he agreed blandly, 'I expect that was it.' Turning away, he walked to the bathroom door, and, to her utter astonishment, removed his shirt and hung it on the hook.

'What the hell do you think you're doing now?' she demanded in alarm.

'Going to shampoo your hair, of course.'

'Don't be so ridiculous! I can do it myself!'

'One-handed?' he asked mildly. 'Stop cutting off your nose to spite your face.'

'I'm doing no such thing! I don't want you in here!' And she didn't, but not from any reasons of modesty, she discovered, her cheeks burning. The sight of his naked chest had set up all sorts of alarming notions and she discovered to her horror that she wanted him in the bath with her. Had thought that was what he intended when he removed his shirt. 'No, Kiel,' she whispered weakly as he returned to kneel beside the bath.

'Yes, Justine,' he argued softly. 'Relax and enjoy. You can always lean forward to hide your—er—attributes, if that's what's bothering you.'

It wasn't, but it might be safer for him to believe that, then she shivered involuntarily when he poured shampoo on to her hair and his large hands began to massage gently.

'Nice?' he queried softly.

'Yes,' she mumbled, 'and don't get it in my eyes!' she warned. She didn't think it would be at all wise to let him know that she was enjoying it, but it was nice. The feel of his strong fingers on her scalp, thumbs, whether inadvertently or not, probing the hollows in her nape, sent a delicious shiver through her, melting her bones. Taking the bar of fragrant soap from the ledge, he began lathering her back and shoulders.

Feeling she ought to protest, she said weakly, 'You don't need to do this.'

'No, but it's nice though, isn't it?' he asked outrageously, then added even more outrageously, 'Besides, I'm enjoying it, and, if you're honest, so are you.' Leaning forward, he whispered in her ear, 'Aren't you?'

'Yes,' she managed, sounding stifled. She felt she could have sat there all day allowing him to massage her stiff muscles, but did he have any idea what he was doing to her pulse-rate? It was also ridiculous to pretend an insouciance she was certainly not feeling, as though it were quite a common occurrence for men to wander casually into her bathroom and proceed to wash her hair. It also seemed highly unlikely that he didn't know exactly what he was doing to her. How would he react, she wondered, if she suddenly pulled him down into the bath with her? Only she had the horrible feeling that it wasn't a lesson that would teach him anything he didn't already know.

With a groan, she pushed her face more firmly into her knees as she tried to stifle the erotic thoughts that were playing havoc with her equilibrium. When he unhooked the shower-head to rinse the suds away, she breathed more easily. Hopefully the torment was nearly over.

'Better?' he asked gently, and, when she looked up to agree, he dropped a light, fleeting kiss on her nose. 'Don't sit there too long getting cold,' he admonished as he got to his feet. Flexing his muscles, as though they were stiff, he walked across to collect his shirt, and, without a backward glance, left.

Letting her breath out in a whoosh, feeling weak and shivery, she quickly finished washing. So now you know, Justine. The sight of your naked body didn't affect him one iota. Getting out, she dried herself quickly and put on her robe as though covering her body would negate its feelings, stop the frustration and need. Running a brush through her hair without looking at herself, perhaps afraid of what she might see in her eyes, she walked into the bedroom and sat by the window to let the breeze dry her hair.

He must never know, she decided, that he could affect her so. To be the object of his amusement would be horrible. The laughter in his eyes for her odd behaviour to date was one thing. To see pity or dismay for her irrational feelings for him was quite another. Don't fall in love with him, Melly had said, almost as though it had been a foregone conclusion.

Well, she wouldn't join the ranks of the presumably frustrated women who had so far thrown themselves at him. She had too much pride.

Restless, and in no mood to sit staring idly out at the little bay, she got up again. Going into the bathroom, she washed out the sling, then hung it at the window to dry. It looked rather like a flag of truce. Turning irritably away, she lay on the bed and tried to quieten her mind, rest, only images of Kiel kept intruding. Strong muscles, the hard, tanned, fit body hovered tantalisingly in her mind. Strong hands that might touch her, caress her. With a groan, she rolled over on to her face, and gradually, as sounds from the pool slowly diminished, voices faded as people went inside to change for dinner, she slipped into a light sleep.

A light touch on her hair woke her, and, thinking it was probably an insect flown in through the open window, she put up a hand to brush it away. On encountering a warm hand, her eyes flew open in shock. In the dim room, he was an indistinct figure as he perched beside her on the bed, and his green eyes appeared almost black as he gazed down at her.

'Kiel?' she whispered.

'Hi,' he said softly. 'I didn't mean to wake you.'

She turned on to her back, her gaze confused for a moment, and, as she struggled to find reality, her hand lifted to touch his face. Becoming aware of what she was doing, she snatched it back, embarrassed. 'What time is it?' she mumbled to cover her confusion.

Without bothering to consult his watch, he informed her quietly, 'Nearly eight.' Taking her hand, he returned it to his jaw, where her fingers fluttered softly like a trapped butterfly. 'You look quite incredibly wanton,' he added with a slight smile.

She felt incredibly wanton, she discovered; she also felt quite unable to move or speak. Certainly it would be impossible to force words past the blockage in her throat. There was a hard, tight pain in her chest, and a fierce desire sent a flood of warmth to the pit of her stomach. When his fingers touched her throat, she stiffened, then groaned weakly when they trailed slowly, too slowly, to the soft swell of her breast.

'I came back early,' he said huskily, 'the search abandoned almost before it was begun. All I could think about were soft, supple limbs, naked limbs, a curved creamy back, a tantalising glimpse of full breasts.'

His voice was thick as he moved her robe aside to expose them, and Justine's breathing became erratic as he lowered his head to press a soft kiss on one rosy tip. She couldn't stop him. Didn't want to stop him. Would it be so wrong to make love with him? she wondered dazedly. Who would it hurt? Except ultimately herself? She wanted him, fiercely, longingly. She knew he wasn't in love with her, that he wasn't offering a permanent arrangement—how could he be? They barely knew each other, and yet her body called to his, as presumably his did to hers. Did it matter so much that there was only liking? Need?

Moving her hand from his jaw, she laid it on his powerful thigh, a tacit encouragement, and, as the muscles bunched, she felt a heady feeling of exhilaration. With deliberate provocation, she slid her hand slowly upwards across his groin. It was as though it was not she who touched, she who wanted. Crossing the barrier of his belt, up to his hard chest to the buttons of his shirt, she slipped her fingers inside. Hearing his hiss of indrawn breath, she slid the buttons free. Her eyes again locked with his, she spread her palm against his warm flesh.

'I hope to God you're telling me what I think you're telling me,' he said thickly, 'because if you're teasing I think I'd kill you.'

'Not teasing,' she managed jerkily, and then forgot to breathe altogether when he untied the belt of her robe. Her stomach muscles contracted as his hand slid across her flesh, and she moved her hand up to the back of his neck and pulled him down to her. As she arched to meet him, her mouth urgently sought his.

His strong arms cradling her, he slipped the robe from her shoulders and drew her naked form against him.

CHAPTER FIVE

BREATH held as he touched her, her flesh almost burning, Justine released it in a long jerky rush, and then it was no longer dreamlike, but an urgent need in both of them. There was tension in Kiel's muscles as he removed his clothes and laid her back before joining his long naked length to hers on the soft bed. Leaning up on one powerful arm, he allowed his darkened eyes to travel slowly down her length. His palm touched, fingers probed, a tactile pleasure that made her wriggle with frustration. Her own hand learned the shape of a man's back, buttocks, thighs, and she cursed the plaster cast that prevented her holding him as she wanted to.

When his mouth followed where his fingers had led, she gasped and held him closer. When his mouth returned to hers, she allowed him an access that no other man had been given. Gaining confidence, she gave him back kiss for kiss, then parted her thighs and shifted her hips to make it easier for him before throwing back her head to expose her long throat to his searching mouth. Fitting her rhythm to his, her arm tight around his waist, she gave herself up to him, allowed him to dictate the pace, and took incredible pleasure for once in being dominated.

She knew, even as her mind refused rational thought, that he was experienced enough to make any woman feel special, fulfilled. Knew he was holding himself in check until she should reach the same plane as he. Her muscles were locked as she rose to join him on the peak, and both held for a moment before tumbling over the edge. Both, for that one, long moment, completely vulnerable, out of control.

When his weight descended on to her soft curves, she held him for a moment, just revelling in the pleasure he had given her. 'Thank you,' she whispered huskily. Licking the salty perspiration from his neck, she gave a small smile when he shivered.

'Thank you?' he queried as he leaned up to look down into her serene face.

'Mm, thank you, it was beautiful. I'm not very—er—experienced, but if you are ever tempted for a repeat I promise to be better.'

His face registering his complete and utter astonishment, he exclaimed softly, a thread of humour in his voice, 'That's the first time a woman has ever thanked me.'

'Is it?' she asked, startled. 'Oh, well, perhaps they never realised how good you were.'

With a shout of laughter, he hugged her to him. 'Oh, Justine, I don't believe you're real.'

'Why?'

'Because, oh...because you're so delightfully unexpected. Thank you,' he chuckled softly.

'I didn't mean it to be funny,' she reproved.

'I know you didn't,' he soothed. Rolling on to his back, he drew her with him, and, settling her comfortably in the curve of his arm so that her head rested on his chest, the plaster cast disposed awkwardly on his stomach, he continued, 'I think that's the nicest thing anyone has ever said to me. I feel— chuffed.'

He sounded so enormously pleased that she grinned. 'Good, so you should be,' she teased. She felt pretty chuffed herself. And relieved, because it had been a very long time since a man had made love to her. Not that Terry's lovemaking had been anything like this! Terry Maguire, with whom she'd had a brief but unsatisfactory affair when she was nineteen, and who, she realised now, had been a very selfish lover. Not that the soured relationship had been entirely his fault. After her sterile teenage years with Aunt Margaret, she had been ripe and ready to fall in love. Had persuaded herself that it *was* love, because she had so desperately wanted it to be. Only of course it wasn't, and never again had she been tempted to repeat that youthful mistake. Until now.

'What are you thinking about?' he asked softly.

With a faint smile, she shook her head.

'Past loves?' he persisted.

Astonished that he should ask, she gave a rueful grimace. 'Singular.'

'Only one love?' he asked in surprise.

'Mm. What did you think? That I was some sort of floozie?'

'No-o,' he denied slowly, 'just an assumption, when you approved my technique.'

With a gurgle of laughter, she slapped his shoulder. '"Comparisons are odious,"' she reproved loftily.

'Well, seeing as you were the one who made it——'

'I did not! I merely said—it was beautiful,' she concluded lamely.

'And so it was,' he agreed blandly. 'Anyway, I'm conceited enough to know that my performance doesn't need comparison.' Then grinned to show that he was mocking himself as much as her.

'Yes, and therein lies the difference between a boy and a man. Do you ever have self-doubts, Kiel?'

'Not about that, no,' he exclaimed on a laugh. 'Thank goodness.'

'No, I meant in other areas. Your sailing, skiing, whatever.'

'Of course; I wouldn't be human otherwise. Not during the actual doing, because by then I'm committed and whatever errors I may have made, wrong decisions, are too late to undo. I just have to make the best of it. I decide on a course of action, and, whether right or wrong, there's no choice but to go ahead.'

'Yes,' she agreed with complete understanding. 'You're a very positive person, aren't you?'

'Yes, indecision drives me insane. That's why I'm so hard on David, I think. If he would only stick to his decisions, I could admire him, appreciate the effort he had given, even if he was wrong. You have to have the courage of your convictions, otherwise no one would ever do anything. You should understand that. You're a positive force.'

'Mm, that's why I got so impatient with Katia.'

'Oh, Katia,' he said humorously. 'She's the original negative. How I came to have such a sister I'll never know. I must admit she drives me insane at times.'

'And yet you had the moulding of her when your father died, didn't you? I seem to remember David saying so.'

'Yes, she was only nine when he died, and I suppose I felt it incumbent upon me to be a sort of father figure.'

'Maybe that's the trouble,' she said cautiously. 'It might have been better if you'd allowed her more independence, let her stand on her own two feet.'

'Allowed?' he asked drily.

'Made, then. She'll never learn to be independent if you solve all her problems for her.'

'I know that,' he sighed. 'The trouble is, without being totally ruthless I'm not sure how to go about it. She will weep so! I thought when she married my problems would be at an end.'

'Only they doubled,' she commiserated with a grin. 'Never mind.' Obeying a strong impulse, she kissed him again. Lowering her mouth to his, she pushed her fingers into the thick springy hair, but as he held her close to deepen the kiss she broke free, teasing, 'If we are going to find David, hadn't we better make a start?'

Groaning, he reluctantly agreed. 'There's always tonight,' he added provocatively.

His words were both comforting and exciting, and as she got reluctantly to her feet she stood for a moment looking down at him. The moon shining through the window silvered his body for moment, an added delight. With his arms beneath his head, she could see properly for the first time what a magnificent male specimen he was. Hard to believe they were now lovers. Yet she didn't feel guilty at what they had done, felt no shame whatsoever, only a spreading warmth and joy, at pleasure given and received. Smiling at him, she padded into the bathroom to wash.

When she returned, he was standing at the window. He was still naked, and desire flickered through her again. She wanted to walk up behind him, hold that strong body in her arms. She wanted so many things, she thought on a sigh. Everything seemed to have moved so fast, out of control. From merely being attracted to him, she now wanted more, and that was dangerous.

Turning to give her a warm smile, he explained, 'I was just watching the fishing-boats putting out to sea.'

'And wishing you were with them?' she asked softly.

'Perhaps. Maybe I'll come back one day, look round properly. I'd like to go to Pico do Arieiro where apparently you can look right down into the crater of the old volcano. See the vine terraces. How the hell they harvest them on those steep slopes is beyond me.' With a baffled shake of his head, he pulled on his trousers, collected the rest of his clothes, and went out.

Standing where he had left her, she tried to throw off the melancholy his words had brought. She hadn't missed the singular. Not 'we' will come back, but 'I', and she wondered if he had done so deliberately, as a warning. Don't fall in love with him. No. It really *was* only attraction. Wasn't it?

Taking the only dress she had brought with her from the wardrobe, she struggled into its soft folds. The loose Indian print was ideal for warm evenings, and the wide sleeves perfect to accommodate the cast. The lacing at the neck could be left open or closed, and, unable to wear a bra, or at least not wishing to ask Kiel to fasten it for her, she wore only a pair of lace panties. Pushing her feet into thonged sandals, she applied a light make-up, brushed her hair, and left it loose.

When Kiel returned for her, having changed into a short-sleeved cream shirt and grey trousers, he gave her a long, comprehensive glance, before grinning wickedly. 'The thought of you wearing nothing but a pair of panties beneath that is not guaranteed to give me a very peaceful evening.'

'Can you see through it?' she exclaimed worriedly. Giving Kiel ideas was one thing. Giving them to half the male population of Madeira was quite another.

'No,' he reassured her, 'but the knowledge is more than enough. Come on, temptress, before I forget my good intentions.'

When they reached the lift, he halted, patted his pockets, gave a comical grimace, and explained. 'It would help to have money. Go on down, I'll meet you in the foyer.'

Going obediently down to the ground floor, she smiled to herself. His possessive tone was an added enchantment. Or it was at the moment; she knew herself well enough to know that total possession, if not tempered with consideration, would be impossible to withstand.

The manager was in Reception, and, giving him a friendly smile, she settled herself to wait. Much to her surprise, he walked across to her. 'You are enjoying your stay, *senhora*?'

'Very much. It's a beautiful hotel.'

'*Sim*. Please do not hesitate to ask for anything you might need. It is unfortunate that you have the broken arm.'

'Yes.' And, because she had nothing else to do, she began in her friendly way to explain just why it was unfortunate, which led to other exchanges, and, before she quite knew where she was, they were chatting animatedly away like old friends. Suddenly catching sight of Kiel, she broke off what she had been saying, and, with a smiling apology, walked across to her companion.

'Sorry, have you been waiting long?'

'Oh, ages,' he said as he took her arm. 'Have I been supplanted in your affections already?'

'No,' she laughed. 'I was just talking to the manager about bookings. Because of the gentle climate, quite a few people come out for winter breaks.'

As they walked up the slight incline to the road, she continued, 'Curiously enough, very few English come here, which is a pity. It's something they'd like to encourage, which makes a nice change,' she added wryly. 'Most countries seem to dislike the English. Or holidaymakers at least.'

'Norwegians don't,' he denied with a smile. 'On the contrary, our countries have very close ties.' His humorous tone left her in no doubt that he was referring to themselves.

Warmed by his bantering tone, she tucked her hand into his arm. 'Apparently, there's even a golf course. Pity we haven't more time; I'd have liked to see it.'

'Justine,' he exclaimed in mock exasperation, 'we are not here as reps for your company!'

'I know, I know, but if there is an opportunity it might be too good to miss. Besides, you'd have gone out with the fishing-boats if you'd had the chance, wouldn't you?' she teased.

'True. I've never been trawling for swordfish. Maybe I'll get up early tomorrow to watch them unload. If I'm not too tired,' he added pointedly.

Glad that the darkness hid her blush, she squeezed the fingers that were now tangled in hers. Happy and at ease, she felt proud when she noticed other women admiring him, envying her, and she grinned, feeling very proprietorial. They hadn't been into the town before, or at least she hadn't; Kiel seemed to know where he was going, and she promised herself that before she left she would come down for a look around.

The little shops nestling closely together in the cobbled alleys looked enticing, and would definitely bear further investigation. As in all the places they'd been so far, there was the cobbled square, the focal point of the towns and villages. The little church—she laughed delightedly when the bell sounded with a dull thonk. Quite obviously cracked. The little blue and white bandstand stood drunkenly beside an enormous tree, and she enjoyed a mental picture of the local band playing, all with a list to starboard.

There seemed a simplicity about Madeira, a gentleness. Despite the obvious signs of poverty, everyone seemed content. They had an old-world courtesy and charm that seemed sadly lacking at home. Like Kiel, she would like to come back one day.

'Why are you smiling?' he asked softly.

Turning to look up at him, she saw the warmth in his eyes, and her smile died, to be replaced by a dryness in her throat, a quickening of her pulse.

'Just enjoying the scenery,' she whispered.

Halting with mutual unspoken consent, they stared at one another, until, with a little groan, he turned her round and urged her back in the direction from which they had just come.

'Where are we going?'

'Back to the hotel.'

'But why?' she asked in bewilderment, and felt a funny little shiver go through her at the expression on his face.

'You know why,' he accused throatily. 'We'll eat at the hotel.'

She hardly needed a crystal ball to know his meaning. He wanted her, and certainly she wasn't averse. There seemed to be a raw hunger inside her for this large Norseman. Had all those years of celibacy made her wanton? Glancing at him from the corner of her eyes, she wondered if that was what he would think. Opportunism? And Melly's words about all those women throwing themselves at his feet came back to haunt her. Only how was she to explain her rather muddled thoughts? That, much as she wanted him, she didn't want him to think her promiscuous? That she wanted him to respect her too? She had told him that there hadn't been anyone for a long while, so wouldn't he think, if she was too eager, too compliable, that...? Allowing her thoughts to tail off in confusion, she sighed. And, even if she tried to explain, how could he possibly be expected to understand her hesitation now, when she had hardly been reticent before? She'd practically thrown herself into his arms! And in the bath. He must have known of her feelings then. Was that why? she wondered in renewed anguish. Because he thought her easy? No, she couldn't believe that. He wasn't in love with her, she knew that, but he did like her, didn't he? Having thrown caution to the winds, how could she now reverse it? Did she even want to reverse it? And the answer to that had to be no.

'What's wrong?' he asked gently, as he directed her into the dining-room and the table they had occupied that morning. 'You've been sighing and muttering to yourself all the way up from the town.'

'Nothing,' she denied brightly, too brightly. Giving him a smile that she hoped hid the ridiculous agitation she was feeling, she hoped he would leave it there. She might have known better.

His eyes slightly narrowed on her bewildered face, he asked neutrally, 'Cold feet, Justine?'

'No!' Catching his disbelieving glance, she gave a funny little gesture of self-mockery. 'Yes, I didn't want you to think I was—er...'

'Easy?' he asked helpfully.

'Yes,' she admitted in relief.

'That's important to you? My opinion?' he asked carefully.

'Yes.' Determined to be totally honest, even if it meant she slept alone, or he returned to his former distant behaviour, she explained haltingly, 'After my—er—behaviour in the bath, I thought you might think I had...engineered the whole thing.'

'I didn't,' he denied. Watching her steadily, his eyes seemingly empty of understanding, or compassion for her predicament, he continued, 'But it's hardly flattering to imply that I can be manipulated. That any woman, whoever she might be, has only to crook her little finger.'

'No!' she exclaimed, horrified, 'I didn't mean that! I didn't, Kiel. Oh, hell, I don't know what I do mean. I just didn't want you to think I was promiscuous,' she concluded lamely.

'I didn't. I thought that, like me, you felt an attraction, a need...'

'I did! Do! I'm sorry,' she mumbled awkwardly. Embarrassed, she began crumbling the roll on her plate into messy crumbs.

'Look at me,' he commanded softly.

Taking a deep breath, she did so, then gave a small shamefaced smile at the look he was giving her. 'I made rather a muck of that, didn't I?'

'A very thorough muck,' he agreed. Picking up the bottle of wine the waiter had brought, and overriding her protest that she wasn't supposed to drink, he filled her glass with slow deliberation. 'I doubt one glass will do you any harm.' When he had filled both glasses, he picked his up, and, his mouth hovering tantalisingly on the rim of the glass, he toasted her.

Her breath lodging somewhere in her throat, and wondering how on earth such a simple act could make her feel so wanton, she picked up her own glass and returned the salute. Averting her eyes, she stared blankly down at the fried banana that decorated the piece of fish that she supposed she must have ordered. *Espada*; swordfish. She vaguely recalled that she had been intending to have fish because it would be easy to eat one-handed, but didn't actually recall ordering it. Eating in public was something she hadn't actually considered in the hospital, and she prayed she wouldn't make a mess of it. She was also very aware of Kiel watching her, and she protested in acute embarrassment, 'Don't.'

'Don't what?' he asked huskily.

'Watch me.' Flicking her eyes up, then hastily away again, she took a panicky sip of wine to ease the dryness in her throat. Tension seemed to be crackling between them like an invisible thread, and, abandoning her glass, she picked up her fork, and began to break the meal up into small pieces, which she then found almost impossible to swallow.

After a long pause, which stretched Justine's nerves almost to breaking point, he said softly, 'Do you actually want that? You've been chasing the poor fish round and round your plate for the last five minutes.'

Gratefully abandoning the attempt to force it past the blockage in her throat, she lay down her fork. Picking up her glass, she recklessly tossed the remainder of the wine back, then held out the empty glass for more.

Holding her eyes, he shook his head. 'I want you sober, and very, very aware of what I'm going to do to you, with you—and for you.'

'Oh, God.' His low throaty chuckle was hardly guaranteed to make her feel any better and she allowed her arm to drop limply back to the table. The warmth spreading through her was almost a pain, and she wriggled uncomfortably in her chair. When Kiel got to his feet, she stared up at him as though mesmerised.

'Up,' he commanded softly.

Standing, she preceded him from the restaurant and into the lift. He didn't touch her; he didn't need to, his eyes on hers were more than enough. Their lovemaking earlier had been spontaneous, almost dreamlike, as she'd woken from sleep. This was deliberate arousal, an assault of mind and senses, and when he courteously indicated she should go ahead of him from the lift she stumbled, and would have fallen if he had not been there to steady her. When he closed the bedroom door behind them with a soft little click, she jumped. He pulled her towards him, one arm encircled her waist while the other untangled the tie at her neck. And his eyes never once left hers.

'I won't pretend that I'd be able to walk away without a qualm if you said no, but I would do it,' he said seriously.

'I know,' she whispered. And she did. He wasn't some callow youth without control, although she wished in some ways that he were; maybe then she wouldn't feel so lacking in confidence.

'And not because I don't want you,' he added tauntingly as he pulled her tight against him, 'because I do. Very much.'

She could feel for herself how much he wanted her, and, on a choked intake of breath, she slid her arm up around his neck. Intending to press closer, she groaned in frustration when the plaster cast prevented her.

Grinning, he chided gently, 'It doesn't matter; there will be other times after it's removed.'

'Will there?' she asked huskily. Knowing very well that her earlier bravado about its only being a beautiful memory was just so much rubbish, she leaned her head against his strong shoulder. All her resolutions were crumbling like sandstone, and there now seemed a very real danger of her falling in love with him, and that would bring only heartache. But she couldn't deny him, or herself; desire was raging too strongly to draw back now. When he untied the sling and dropped it to the floor, then turned his attention to carefully removing her dress, she gave up thinking any thoughts at all.

Sliding his palms up her back and round to her shoulders, he bent his head to kiss her, and then, a faint smile in his eyes, he picked her up and carried her to the bed. 'Make love to me, Justine,' he persuaded softly. 'Give me all the fire you denied me earlier,' and then proceeded to start a fire of his own as he trailed provocative kisses from her neck to her navel. His thumbs a warm torment on the insides of her thighs, he removed the last barrier to his seeking mouth. From that moment, Justine allowed instinct to take over. Teasing and dominant by turn, she revelled in the feeling of power, until exhaustion claimed them and they slumped tiredly against each other. The gentle breeze through the open window was pleasantly cool on their heated flesh.

His mouth pressed to her throat, he murmured thickly, 'If that's what you can do to me with one arm in plaster, I don't dare contemplate what you could do without it.'

A pleasant languor filling her, she trailed her fingers along his spine, and let out a long, contented breath.

Levering himself up, so that he could look down into her face, he asked quietly, 'Why the sigh?'

'For pleasure given and received,' she said simply. 'For a feeling of completeness. For a super man who makes me feel special. For—oh, for everything.'

'You're not so bad yourself,' he complimented with a wide grin. With a hard, deep kiss, he lay down and hugged her to his side.

Grateful, and happy that he didn't seem to intend to rush away, back to his own room, she closed her eyes and snuggled contentedly against him. The unfamiliar warmth of someone beside her was a delight, and she closed her mind to thoughts of all the tomorrows and was unaware that he watched her for a while, his feelings every bit as confused as her own.

When she woke, yawning widely, she hoisted herself carefully into a sitting position, so that she could watch him. His lashes were long for a man, slightly darker than his hair. Obeying a strong impulse, she traced his straight, arrogant nose, with her finger, then smiled when he grunted and twitched in his sleep. The stubble on his chin rasped against her palm and she moved her hand to his broad tanned shoulder to touch the powerful muscles in his back. He really was a magnificent animal, and, for a moment, she fantasised that he would fall in love with her, give her the right to wake in his bed each morning. Smoothing the tousled hair back from his forehead, she sighed. It was far too late to tell herself she was immune to his charm; she wasn't immune at all. Extraordinary as it seemed after their disastrous beginning, she liked him too much. His moodiness, his smiles...and a fat lot of good that will do you, Justine. 'Don't come running to me when you get hurt,' Melly had said. Well, I won't, she promised silently again. Whatever the outcome, she would run to no one. And, if she got hurt, she would only have herself to blame.

Easing herself from the bed, using the pillow to replace her thigh beneath his head, she was thoroughly disconcerted when he opened his eyes and gazed blankly at her for a moment before recognition dawned.

'Sneaking away?' he asked with a grin.

'I was considering it, yes,' she agreed with a faint smile of her own. Hovering uncertainly, embarrassed by her nakedness, she had the decision taken out of her hands.

'Not allowed,' he rumbled. Rolling on to his back, he captured her hand and pulled her to lie on top of him. With a grunt of pain as the plaster cast caught him in the ribs, he eased her into a more comfortable position. 'How long have you got to wear that thing?'

'Five weeks,' she said gloomily.

'By which time I'll be black and blue. Oh, well, where there's a will, there's a way.' Turning sideways, he gave her a swift kiss. 'Good morning.'

Unable to repress the grin that tugged at her mouth, she commented, 'You look like a very unsavoury pirate.'

Rasping his chin against her soft cheek, he murmured provocatively, 'Don't you like pirates, Justine?'

'Oh, yes, sometimes I like them very much. Too much, perhaps,' she added softly. Lifting her arm, she threaded her fingers through his tousled hair with sensuous enjoyment.

'Can one like someone too much?' he queried huskily.

'Oh, yes.' Searching his eyes, she asked quietly, 'Why?'

'Why am I attracted to you?' When she nodded, he moved back a fraction so that he could see her face properly. 'I don't know,' he admitted wryly. Tracing one finger across her features, he smiled. 'You aren't at all in the mould of the females that usually attract me. In fact, when I saw you in the hospital...'

'You thought me as prickly as a hedgehog with the morals of an alleycat,' she finished for him.

'Well, not precisely an alleycat,' he teased, 'but certainly prickly.'

'And whose fault was that, might I ask? You only ever reap what you sow,' she pointed out piously. Watching him, examining the wicked glitter in his beautiful dark green eyes, she asked with morbid curiosity, 'What sort of women do attract you?' Not that she really wanted to know, but it might help resolve the doubts and confusion that kept surfacing. It might also clarify why he'd wanted to make love to herself. Thinking about it on a rational level, it seemed quite extraordinary. 'Dumb blondes?' she asked lightly.

'Now why should you assume that? Or even say it in that disparaging tone, I wonder?'

'I don't know,' she shrugged, 'it seems the sort most men prefer, for—er—liaisons.'

'Nonsense! A man doesn't only want a woman for her looks, or, conversely, for her mind. Even sexual gratification needs something more than a body. Some "dumb blondes", as you call them, can be amusing, or, at the other end of the scale, those with, say, a Mensa mentality can be extremely boring. It's certainly not the degree of intelligence, although it is nice to be able to converse,' he added humorously.

'So why me?' she persisted.

'God knows,' he laughed. 'None of the other women I've known seem to last more than a few weeks, yet almost against my will I find myself liking you. Maybe it's your quicksilver changes of mood that intrigue me. Maybe it's the fact that when you laugh, or become animated, you're almost beautiful. On the other hand,' he argued with a crooked grin, 'it might be your funny little nose, or those extraordinary eyes that are sometimes rather disconcertingly direct, like now. But, whatever the reason, I do like you. Rather more than I want to,' he concluded with bitter honesty. 'You seem to have crept in under my guard when I wasn't looking.'

Which was hardly comforting, she thought. Only, because he seemed to think she was taking it in the same spirit as himself, pride insisted he didn't see otherwise. Tweaking his nose, she scrambled to her feet and went into the bathroom to shower.

So now you know, Justine; it's a light-hearted flirtation, nothing more. And, if you're really lucky, it might last all of two weeks. How disgustingly weak-willed of her to allow him to use her. ''Tis better to have loved and lost than never to have loved at all,' she quoted as she awkwardly rinsed herself off— and whoever had written *that* needed his head examined! And telling herself that maybe she was the one to make him forsake all others was as self-deluding as it was ridiculous! What she should do was tell him to take a hike—only she quite desperately didn't want to do that. Caught in a web of her own making, what the hell did she do when he loosened the silken strands? Cry? Because he would loosen them, of that, there was no doubt.

CHAPTER SIX

AFTER breakfast, which they both ate hungrily, they walked hand in hand across the headland with the intention of going into town to get a taxi and resume their search. Stopping almost simultaneously, they turned to stare out over the bay. When Kiel put his arm round Justine, she turned to give him a faint smile. 'You didn't get to see the fishing fleet come back after all.'

'No, I had better things to do.' Dropping a light kiss on her nose, he pulled her down to sit on the bank.

'We're supposed to be looking for David,' she pointed out.

'I know; we'll look later.'

'How much later?' she teased.

'Much, much later,' he promised. With a smooth motion, he rolled over and captured her mouth with his.

Abandoning the struggle with her conscience, and her half-formed determination to keep him at a distance, she gave herself up to the pleasure of his touch like a miser after gold. Kissing him fiercely, she tried to recapture their earlier light-heartedness, but it was without very much success. Minutes now were precious, time counted as it ticked away, and she tried very hard not to visualise their eventual parting. Kiel Lindstrom was a man she would find it very difficult to forget.

When they eventually made a move, they went to the restaurant they had used before, and when they had eaten the delicious lamb kebabs both leaned back replete. Kiel's gaze was fixed on her face, and she gave a faint sigh. How was it, she wondered, that everything seemed brighter, cleaner, the sky more blue, when she was with him?

'You've got freckles,' he suddenly announced.

Wrinkling her nose at him, she put her hand up to cover them. 'Hateful things—the sun brings them out.'

'They're beautiful, adorable, like everything else about you.'

'Everything?' she queried in disbelief. Raising her eyebrows queryingly in imitation of his own, she desperately fought to keep things in perspective.

'Well, nearly everything,' he qualified as he eyed the plaster cast. 'And, reluctant as I am, I suppose we had better make a move.'

They spent the rest of the afternoon looking around the town, poking into shops, trying on the Madeiran caps with much giggling on Justine's part. Kiel looked utterly ridiculous in one of the traditional hats that most of the older men sported. The black felt-like material, decorated with colourful embroidery, and long ear-flaps, made him look like Deputy Dawg.

'I like Deputy Dawg,' he retorted in mock affront. 'I'm going to buy one; it will keep my ears warm when I'm sailing.'

'You can't!' she protested laughingly. 'Whatever will your crew think?'

Looking at her in astonishment, he demanded, 'Why on earth should I care what my crew think?'

Unable to think of a satisfactory answer, she shook her head at him, but the mental picture of him wearing such outrageous headgear had her in stitches. She was still chuckling when they left the shop and made their way to the town square. The plan was to have a drink in each of the bars in the hope of seeing David, but they were distracted so many times by the goods on display in the little shops that it all took a great deal longer than expected. Kiel wanted to buy an embroidered tablecloth for Melly. Justine wanted some of the lace-work, which necessitated a long hunt through the local emporium, which sold a great many other things, which all had to be examined. When they finally reached the square, both were extremely thirsty, and, on Justine's part at least, tired and footsore.

Her pleasure in his company was also tinged by sadness, as she wondered if this was all she would have. Yet she couldn't regret their affair. Kiel was the most exciting and attractive man she had ever met;

it was a once in a lifetime thing. Whatever you took in this life, you paid for, or so Aunt Margaret had always been so fond of quoting, yet it was true—she would pay for this, and it was no good pretending otherwise. But if they could find David tonight she and Kiel could at least have one last full day together, to do with as they pleased. Feeling more cheered by the prospect, she quickened her pace.

Wrangling amiably over whose fault it was it had taken so long to reach the square, they pushed through the bead curtain of the first bar they came to. 'You were the one who insisted on looking at the wine ra—— Oh, my goodness,' she exclaimed weakly. 'It's David.' Halting in shock, unable to believe that they had actually found him, she stared at the tall, fair-haired man leaning against the bar, and, because it now seemed that her plans for the next day would bear fruit, she greeted him delightedly.

Much to her astonishment, instead of looking surprised, he grinned and exclaimed in satisfaction, 'I knew you'd change your mind!'

Thoroughly nonplussed, she said weakly, 'What?'

Ignoring her bewilderment, he advanced, arms held wide, then halted comically as he noticed the plaster cast. 'Good grief, woman, what on earth have you done?'

'I crashed your car,' she admitted sheepishly.

'You did what?' His expression rapidly changing from pleasure to horror, he demanded, 'How bad is it?'

Knowing very well that he wasn't talking about her arm, she exclaimed in exasperation, 'David! You could at least try for some concern for me first! Even if it wasn't genuine, it would at least be a sop to my pride to think that I was more important than your wretched car.'

With a grimace, which Justine was sure wasn't caused by contrition, he asked quickly, 'How are you?'

'Fine,' she said, laughing. 'Broken wrist and concussion. Thank you for asking.' Then, on impulse, she leant forward to drop a light kiss on his cheek. David never changed; she didn't suppose he ever would. David's concerns were always of far more importance than anyone else's. 'But why aren't you surprised to see——?'

'Do you think,' Kiel enunciated coldly from behind them, 'that you could continue your mutual enchantment at a later date?'

His sneering tone was like a douche of cold water, and, swinging round, Justine looked at him in confusion.

'What the hell are you doing here?' David demanded in shock.

'Looking for you.'

'Why?' Then obviously finding his own answer, he exploded, 'Katia! I might have known you'd be still wet-nursing her! Well, I wish you'd keep your nose out of my affairs!'

'I would be more than delighted to do so, believe me, if your "affairs" didn't keep intruding into my life. However, in this instance, I am not here on Katia's behalf, merely for the plans. So if you will give them to me I'll leave.'

'Plans? What plans?'

'The plans you took from John's desk. The plans for Challenger which have to be presented on Monday morning.'

'What? But I haven't got them!'

'You must have them! They were on John's desk before you made your whirlwind appearance. When you'd gone, so had the plans!'

'But I didn't take them! Well, I did,' he qualified sulkily, 'but not on purpose.' Swinging round on a startled Justine, who was wondering how everything had suddenly degenerated into a shouting match, he demanded, 'Why on earth didn't you give them to him?'

'Me?' she squealed in astonishment. 'How did I get involved in this? I don't have the damned plans!'

Staring at her in disbelief, he burst out, 'Don't be ridiculous! I gave them to you!'

'You did not!'

'Justine,' he said with awful patience, 'I gave them to you. When you got into the car to drive with me to the airport, they were on the seat, bundled up with my life-jacket. I gave them to you, and you took them indoors for safety.'

Staring at him, her eyes almost violet, she felt suddenly sick. She didn't dare look at Kiel, his very stillness told her all she needed to know about his feelings. 'What did I do with them?' she whispered.

'Oh, God.' Raking one hand through his hair, he sighed deeply. 'I don't know. I asked you to make sure that John got them back. I explained what they were, and you took them indoors.'

Searching her mind, and finding only blankness, she continued to stare helplessly at him, until he burst out irritably, 'Oh, come on, Justine, you must remember! It was only a few days ago, for goodness' sake! You know how important they are; stop playing games!'

'I'm not playing games,' she insisted, distressed. 'I'm not!'

'Well, think!'

'She is thinking,' Kiel put in coldly, 'and, believe me, badgering her into trying to remember will produce nothing more profitable than a waspish tongue—and if she'd had any memory of it we'd hardly have come chasing out here to look for you, would we?'

'Shut up, Kiel!' David snapped. 'She's not a geriatric!' Turning back to Justine, he began coaxingly, 'Now, I gave you the plans, you——'

'David,' Kiel interrupted with heavy patience, 'Justine does not remember, because she's lost her memory of events just prior to the accident, and for some hours after it.'

'What?' Swivelling towards Justine, he demanded, 'Is that true?' When she nodded miserably, he burst out, 'Well, why didn't you say so in the first place?'

'I did!' Belatedly registering the attention they were attracting, she asked listlessly, 'Do you think we could continue this discussion somewhere more private?'

'What? Oh, hell,' he muttered in disgust as he too registered the curious faces around them. 'Hang on, I'll settle my bill, then we'll go along to the villa.'

As David walked back to the bar, she followed Kiel outside, miserably aware of his cold withdrawal. She hadn't missed his taunt about an affair, either, and needed very much to know what he was now so busily thinking.

'What was that nasty little dig about an affair?' she asked him rather belligerently.

Leaning back against the wall, folding his arms across his chest, he gave an indifferent little shrug.

'Tell me,' she insisted stormily.

'There's nothing to tell,' he denied distantly. 'I merely said I wasn't interested in his affairs.'

'Meaning you think David and I are having one.'

Turning his head, he gave her back glare for glare. 'Just leave it alone, will you?'

'No! I want you to tell me! Is it because of the plans? Is that why you're so cross?'

'No, it isn't because of the bloody plans! I don't like being made a fool of! And, with someone you insist is only your stepcousin, you seem very, very chummy!'

'I wasn't chummy! I was being normally friendly!' Her own temper rising to match his, she insisted, 'I told you before, there's nothing between us!'

'How do you know?' he asked silkily. 'You don't remember.'

'Oh, don't be so stupid! If we weren't having an affair on Sunday morning, which I remember very clearly, we could hardly be having one by Sunday afternoon! Unless there was a passionate conflagration during my cooking of the lunch,' she added sarcastically, 'which even you have to admit is highly unlikely.'

'Do I?' he asked distastefully. 'But then you'd only really known me for forty-eight hours before our "passionate conflagration",' he sneered bitingly. 'You've known David for fifteen years! And for your information, his flight didn't leave Gatwick until eleven-thirty at night—plenty of time after the roast beef, I would have thought.'

'You bastard!' she gasped in disbelief. Drawing back her hand, she lashed out for his cheek, only to have her wrist captured in his powerful fist before she could connect. Grinding her teeth in fury, she spat, 'Got it all worked out, haven't you? All cut and dried! I *told* you there was nothing between us!'

'You told me any number of things,' he said with sneering distaste. Turning away as though he could no longer bear the sight of her, he was wrenched back by Justine's furious assault on his arm.

'And you believed none of them?' she demanded.

Shrugging his arm from her hold, his face back to the distant mask that had so infuriated her in the hospital, he retorted coldly, 'No, why should I?'

'Even when we were making love?' she persisted, needing to know it all. Have it clear, straight from his mouth. No innuendo, no half-truths, but clear honesty, no matter how sick it made her feel.

'Having sex,' he corrected icily. 'There is a difference.'

'I know there's a damned difference!' she snapped.

'Then why so surprised? You surely didn't think I'd fallen passionately in love with you?'

'No, I didn't. Neither did I think you were using me for your sexual gratification! I thought that it had at least been from mutual liking and wanting.'

'Did you? How quaintly old-fashioned,' he sneered. 'And if you hadn't flaunted yourself so blatantly a——'

'Flaunted?' she screeched. 'Flaunted?'

'Yes, flaunted. I'm only human.'

'Oh, no, Kiel,' she derided harshly, 'you're not human at all. You are a cold, calculating bastard.'

'Which makes you what?' he asked nastily. 'Think I missed his little gibe about expecting you? Pity you didn't remember to tell him that your liaison was a secret.'

With no way of explaining until she had spoken to David, she looked away. Hearing the bead curtain rattle as David came out, she turned her back on both men to give herself time to gain a measure of control.

'I'll see if I can get us an earlier flight back to England,' Kiel retorted coldly.

Giving him a look of loathing, she saw that his green eyes were colder than the Norwegian water that he loved so much, his face as carved as the mountains.

'Arrogant bastard,' David muttered as Kiel strode off. Taking her arm, he urged her into motion, 'Come on, my villa's just along here.'

As soon as she saw the villa, she remembered it, and, preceding him into the lounge, she collapsed weakly into the only chair, as though all her energy had drained away. All she could see was Kiel's cold face, the contempt in his eyes.

'You'd better explain,' David said wearily. Standing facing her, his hands pushed into his trouser pockets, he asked disbelievingly, 'Do you really not remember anything?'

'No,' she denied woodenly. 'The last thing I remember is cooking Sunday lunch. I don't remember you coming. I don't remember driving with you to the airport.'

'Or presumably crashing my car,' he added moodily.

'Oh, for God's sake! Is that all you can think of? You leave Katia, who incidentally has been accusing me of trying to steal you—at your instigation, I might add!' She felt no satisfaction at all when he went red. 'You take the plans that might rescue your company from ruin—and it's no good telling me you gave them to me,' she retorted quickly when he opened his mouth to protest. 'They were your responsibility, and all you can ask about is your rotten car!'

'Well, it was practically new! And I certainly can't afford to replace it until this order goes through!'

'If it goes through,' she corrected.

'All right, if! And what are you shouting at me for? I thought we were friends!'

With a disagreeable little twitch, she asked without much interest, 'Why was I in your car, anyway? I have a perfectly good one of my own.'

'Well, of all the... It was you who insisted we take mine! I asked you to run me to the airport, and you said, in your usual niggling fashion, that you weren't about to use your petrol for a trip that was nothing to do with you! Talk about tight! So we used mine, and look where that got me!' he added aggrievedly.

'All right, all right, no need to go on about it.' Too tired to fight any more, she got slowly to her feet. Her head was aching, and there was a hollow pain inside of her. And if only David would use a bit of gumption now and again a great deal of strife would be avoided. 'It's about time you started facing up to your responsibilities,' she reproved quietly, 'and why in God's name did you have to tell Katia we were lovers?' she burst out crossly. 'I've never heard of anything so damned stupid!'

'Because I was tired of her going on and on about her precious brother! Why couldn't I be more like him? Why couldn't I do all the things he does? I lost my temper,' he said sullenly, 'and told her if she wanted me to be like him I'd get myself a string of women, that I would start with you because you wouldn't give me a hard time! Boy, was that a mistake on my part,' he concluded bitterly.

'Well, what did you expect?'

'I didn't expect you to take Kiel's side!' he shouted petulantly.

'I didn't take his side!'

'A man has some pride, Jus,' he continued as though she hadn't spoken. 'You don't know what it's like, having the great Kiel Lindstrom rammed down your throat every five minutes. Anyway, it serves him right, let him believe that a member of his precious family can't have everything she wants...'

'Which is presumably why you allowed him to think you were expecting me!' she put in wrathfully.

'I was expecting you!' he exclaimed. 'I asked you to come with me, and you said you'd think about it!'

'Presumably because I didn't know then that you'd told Katia we were lovers!'

Ignoring that, he added petulantly, 'And as for bringing him with you——'

'Well, it's not my fault I can't remember!' she snapped resentfully.

'No, I suppose it's not your fault that you slept with him either!'

Staring at him in disbelief, that he of all people could be so nasty, she asked with dangerous softness, 'How do you know?'

'How?' he exclaimed with a disbelieving laugh. 'I should think half of Madeira must have heard you shouting at each other outside the bar!'

'Oh.' Her eyes bleak, she said bitterly, 'It's so easy for you, isn't it? You do exactly as you please, but no one else must have needs, wants. You're so damned selfish! All your life people have cushioned you against reality, first Aunt Margaret, then me, Kiel, even Katia. Well, I don't have any cushions, I only have reality. Do you think I don't need comfort sometimes? Warmth? No, of course you don't. It's all right for men, they can go and find release and no one bats an eyelid. A woman does the same, and she's immediately branded a tramp! Well, I wanted him, damn you! Wanted him to make love to me!' When he only continued to stare at her as though she were a deranged stranger, she gave a choked little laugh. She wanted to weep for his selfishness, his unconcern for her needs. 'I shall need some money for the taxi fare,' she stated coldly, 'then you can go back to your insular little life, your cosy indifference to other people's needs.'

With a speed that was insulting, he took some money from his pocket and pushed it at her. 'Where are you staying?'

'Machico. The Dom Pedro.' Wanting only now to escape, be on her own, she turned and left. Tears blurred her vision as she stumbled back to the square.

On the taxi ride back to the hotel, she had ample time to reflect on the disastrous evening. As she went over and over it in her head, her mood gradually changed from self-pity to anger. Why in God's name should she apologise for being human? Why should she feel guilty? She'd done nothing to be ashamed of. And how could David, who had been like a brother to her, be so selfish? Was it so incomprehensible that she had needs? And Kiel. Making her out to be some sort of tramp. In fact, the more she thought about his behaviour, the angrier she became, thought of all the cutting phrases she could have used. Should have used. How dared they treat her as a nothing, a nobody, use her for their gratification? Kiel as a damned tour guide and release for his sexual appetite, David for his own selfish, childish reasons to get back at Kiel and Katia. Well, she was damned if she was going to allow herself to be a shuttlecock batted back and forth between them! How dared Kiel accuse her of being little better than a prostitute? How dared he? Even if that was what he thought, did he have to say so? No, he damned well didn't! And if he thought she was meekly going to accept his insults, he'd soon find out his mistake!

When they halted at the hotel, she thrust all the money David had given her into the startled taxi driver's hand, scrambled out and stormed into Reception. Whisking up to the desk, she demanded her key in a tone that brooked no argument, and certainly didn't encourage the desk clerk to enquire after her evening. Marching across to the lift, she stabbed viciously at the button.

All the way up in the lift, along the corridor, she fumed. Reaching Kiel's door, and seeing that the catch wasn't down, she thrust the door wide with enough energy to crash it back against the wall. Kiel was standing at the window and whirled round at her noisy entrance.

'Get out!' he snarled.

'No!' Jaw set pugnaciously, she stepped into the room and slammed the door behind her. 'You once accused me of needing constant reassurance, continued proof of a man's affections. Well, you were wrong! What I need is honesty! Is that so much to ask? If you wanted a one-night stand, a woman for the moment, then fine. Why not say so? Why the teasing? The kindness? Why the pretence?'

'Because it's what women expect. Isn't it all part of the game?' he sneered.

'Not my game, it isn't!' she snapped. 'I didn't expect declarations of love or undying devotion—how could I? As you so rightly pointed out, we barely knew each other. But I liked you, Kiel, thought you a man of honour, a man of honesty. I *liked* you!' she shouted. 'But to sneer at my feelings, denigrate them, make me out to be a tramp, wasn't honest, wasn't honourable. Even if that was what you thought, there was no need to say it. You tried to cheapen something that for me was special, and for that I can't forgive you. Denigrating that, you only denigrated yourself. Not me. Not ever me! David used me for his own selfish, childish reasons. You used me for yours. I consider that I'm the only one who came out of this with honour,' she said with quiet dignity. Staring at him, searching his face, trying to see behind the mask and failing, she added poignantly, 'It's nice to have a splendid package, a tall straight body, a handsome face, but if the mind, if the feelings don't match, then you're ugly, Kiel, and the package doesn't count. And then I was the fool, for believing different.' With nothing more to say, she turned and quietly left. Going along to her own room, she stood in the dark for long minutes as she desperately fought to keep her mind blank, then jumped at the loud crash that came from his room. It had been loud enough to alert the whole hotel, as though he had thrown something heavy against the wall. Snapping the lock on her door, she undressed, then crawled wide-eyed into bed. I won't feel guilty, she vowed silently. I won't let them make me feel ashamed, or cheap. Rolling on to her face, she cried quietly into the pillow, until exhaustion claimed her, and she slept.

The sunshine next morning was a mockery, but at least gave her the excuse of wearing her sunglasses, which successfully hid the puffiness of her eyes. Dressed in blue cotton trousers and a white T-shirt, she went down to the lobby.

A letter was handed to her as she emerged from the lift. It was a terse note from Kiel, informing her that there were no seats available on an earlier flight, which meant a whole day to get through before they could leave. Screwing the note up, she hurled it into the nearest waste-paper basket and went to have breakfast. Alone. Kiel had either already gone out, or was hiding in his room. Whatever the reason, she was thankful not to meet him. She wished she *never* had to meet him again.

When she left the dining-room, she saw the manager making a beeline towards her. Pretending not to see him, she hurried outside, then reluctantly slowed her pace when she became aware of the curious glances thrown at her. Walking down to the town, she fulfilled the promise she had made to herself of looking round. Only what should have been a pleasant stroll round the shops became a nightmare of remembering. She didn't see the coloured leather shoes in the shoe shop, despite gazing for endless moments into the window. Her mind didn't take in any of the arts and crafts in the little Aladdin's Cave, despite handling them. As she replaced each item meticulously, her eyes remained blank. Not only was there Kiel's behaviour to contend with, but the fact that she had been responsible for the plans. Yet, try as she might, thinking and thinking until her head throbbed, she had no memory of David giving them to her.

Listlessly making her way to the taxi rank, she half-heartedly returned the greetings from the women sweeping the cobbles in the square. The same taxi driver that she and Kiel had used before was there, and he greeted her cheerfully.

'*Bom dia, senhora.*'

Managing a small smile, she returned, '*Bom dia.*' Recalling something else she had wanted to do, she stood in frowning thought for a moment, before asking hesitantly, '*Pico do Arieiro?*'

'*Sim,*' he agreed happily.

Hoping that was indeed the name of the extinct volcano, she climbed into the cab. Even if it wasn't, it was somewhere, and somewhere was better than wandering aimlessly round trying to pass the time.

Barely before she was settled, he took off, far too fast, throwing Justine back into her seat. With an exclamation of disgust, she scrambled upright, and, catching his wickedly amused eye in the mirror, gave a reluctant snort of laughter. It was pure showing-off, of course, and she wondered if he thought all Englishmen drove at the speed of sound.

He also kept up a constant flow of chatter, not one word of which Justine understood, but at least it helped to keep her mind off Kiel. Not that he seemed bothered that she didn't answer, but she could have wished he'd pay more attention to his driving. He wasn't alone in his vehicular erraticism. No one else seemed to keep to their own side of the road either. Cars wove in and out of each other on whichever side of the road they happened to like best. Or so it seemed, and she was profoundly thankful when they left the main road behind. Or she was initially, until they began the steep climb. Blind bend after blind bend, with her driver—deliberately or otherwise— driving in the centre of the road. With a shudder, she turned her head away and looked from the side- window instead. The tree-line gradually gave way to scrubby grass and rock, and she exclaimed in aston- ishment when she saw sheep grazing.

'*Sim,*' he nodded. '*Borrego*. Only flat place.' Turning round to see if she understood, he merely grinned when she rather horrifiedly indicated for him to watch where he was going. It wasn't so much that his inattention might cause them to run into other cars—there were no other cars on this mountain road—but there were a hell of a lot of ravines he could drive over.

'*Borrego* is lambs?' he queried, this time, thank- fully, conversing with her through the rear-view mirror.

'*Sim,*' she agreed with no very clear idea whether it was or it wasn't.

'Low down, they falls off!' Laughing delightedly at his own wit, and as though encouraged by her interest, he began to point out others.

Gathering that he meant this was the only flat place on the island where sheep could run, or walk, without falling off, she nodded. Although she hadn't seen much of Madeira, she did know that she hadn't seen any flat areas, and presumably sheep, unlike mountain goats, couldn't manage on steep hillsides. A suddenly vivid mental image of sheep, clinging desperately by their finger—or rather hoof—tips, to a crumbling ledge, made her smile; nevertheless, she was extremely thankful when they reached the gravel car park at the top.

Climbing stiffly out, buffeted by the strong wind, she struggled to hold her hair back as she stared in dismay at the brown dusty earth. There were a few stunted trees, the obligatory boulder, and very little else. It looked like a moonscape, a terrible contrast to the lushness below, and she shivered at the sheer emptiness of it all. Her disappointment must have shown on her face, because, with a little chuckle, the taxi driver took her hand and led her past the ramshackle shed selling drinks, and along a narrow, broken path. And there, spread before her in panoramic splendour, were range upon range of mountains. Dark towering peaks thrust upward into the blue sky, piercing the white fluffy clouds that clung to their tips like medieval banners.

'OK?' he asked happily.

'*Sim,*' she agreed. 'OK.'

'You see, I wait.' Indicating back the way they had come, he waited to see if she understood.

Nodding her comprehension, she smiled and turned to negotiate the broken and rocky ground towards the best vantage-point. The clouds swirling round the peaks gave the illusion of movement, as though the rocky crags were swaying, and for a moment she felt giddy. Walking to the edge of the path, she stared down into what had once presumably been the crater of the long-dead volcano. In her mind's eye she saw the glowing heart, red and black and yellow. A viscous liquid that heaved and spat as it rose and spilled inexorably over to snake its way down to the lushness below. Without fear or favour, it would destroy everything in its path. Now, trees clung tenaciously where once molten lava had reigned. Or rained, she thought whimsically. Had anyone ever fallen down there? she wondered. If they had, it would have been almost impossible to climb out unaided, and she took a hasty step backwards, just in case.

Returning her gaze to the peaks, she felt dwarfed. Hard to imagine now the primeval power that had thrust these mighty jagged monoliths up from the earth's crust. Hard to imagine the terrifying splendour; yet what should have held her in awe only

made her feel more dispirited. Turning away, she
began to retrace her steps. Keeping her eyes on her
feet in order to safely negotiate the track, she didn't
look up until she reached the piece of rickety fence,
all that remained of what once had presumably been
a safety barrier, then froze in disbelief. Kiel was
talking to her taxi driver, yet his cold green eyes were
fixed unwaveringly on herself. With a defiant glare,
she sidled past. Unable to march, as she wanted to,
because of the narrowness of the path, and fully
conscious of the fact that one slip and she'd be down
in the crater, she nevertheless went as fast as she
dared. If the taxi driver thought it odd they did not
speak, she didn't care.

Walking back to the car to wait for him, she could
then only stare in disbelief and fury when Kiel came
with him and calmly climbed into the front of the
taxi.

'What the hell do you think you're doing?'

Giving her a look of derision, he calmly replaced
his sunglasses on his nose. 'Getting a lift back to
Machico, what else?' he asked mildly.

'Not in my cab you aren't!' she denied forcefully.
'Go back the way you came!'

'If I were able to go back the way I came, I would
hardly need to share your cab,' he pointed out reasonably. 'Unfortunately, the coach has already de-
parted.'

Vaguely recalling the rather battered blue coach
that had been in the car park when she arrived, she

glared round her as though expecting it to suddenly materialise. When it did nothing so convenient, she said icily, 'Then you will have to wait for alternative transport. You are *not* coming in my cab!'

'Don't be childish,' he reproved with studied indifference. His eyes on hers, he pulled the door to.

Before she could do all the things she wanted to do, like stamp her foot, scream, drag him bodily from the cab, the driver walked up, smiled at her, and climbed behind the wheel. Knowing full well that Kiel was quite capable of telling the man to drive on and leave her behind, she dragged open the rear door and climbed resentfully in. All right, she told herself mutinously, if he wanted to share her cab he could damn well pay for it!

The moment the cab stopped in the square, she climbed out and walked away. If the driver thought her rude, she didn't care. Yes, she did, she admitted miserably. It wasn't his fault that Kiel was such a bastard.

CHAPTER SEVEN

WALKING to the little café she had seen that morning, Justine chose a table in the garden beneath the welcome shade of a large tree. Ordering a coffee, omelette and salad, she ate without interest, her thoughts centred on Kiel, until she ruthlessly banished his image from her mind. She would *not* think about him! She wouldn't! The ache inside would eventually go away. It had to.

When she'd finished, and settled her bill, not knowing what else to do, she walked despondently back to the hotel. Perhaps she would rest for a while. Her head still ached, as if there were a tight band round her temples, but even that plan was thwarted. As she walked into Reception, the manager collared her. He looked as though he had been waiting for her, which he probably had, poor man; it was only natural he would use whatever means he could find to fill his hotel, and, at the moment, she obviously seemed the best bet. It was her own fault; she shouldn't have told him she ran her own travel company. That would teach her to keep her mouth shut.

'*Bom dia*, Miss Hardesty—you have had a pleasant day?'

'Yes, thank you, I went up to the old volcano. It was magnificent,' she added lamely.

'You should go on an island tour while you are here. The vine terraces, the waterfalls, the hot springs. It is a beautiful island.'

'Yes, I know. Unfortunately, I have to return to England tomorrow.'

Looking awkward, and hopeful, and embarrassed, all at the same time, he asked hesitantly, 'Would it be an imposition if I asked to show you my hotel? I do not wish to spoil what little time you have left, but—as you can see, we are nowhere filled to capacity,' he concluded with a helpless little shrug.

'And a manager's job is to manage,' she agreed with a faint smile. 'Very well, I'm sorry if I sound less than enthusiastic—my wretched arm,' she lied.

'Of course. It is unfortunate. It is painful?' he asked with kind concern.

Feeling guilty for lying to this kind man, she mumbled awkwardly, 'It just aches a bit.'

'Then if you are sure...'

'Perfectly sure.' She had nothing else to do, and perhaps it would take her mind off her own troubles.

He showed her over the hotel with a thoroughness which exhausted her, and, when they had finished, he invited her into his office for tea and pastries, an offer she didn't have the heart to refuse. 'You will attend the *fado* singing this evening?'

'*Fado?*'

'*Sim*, it is I think like your folk songs, of the region. Sad, haunting. Isabella Aveira, famous—to us.' He smiled deprecatingly. 'They tell of love, of losing, pain and sorrow. Very sad, very lovely.'

Which was just about all she needed, she thought despondently. 'Where is she singing?' If it was a long way away, she would have a good excuse for refusing, only to have that idea dashed at birth.

'Why, here, of course, in the hotel. In the disco room,' he added with an expressive little grimace, and Justine guessed, quite rightly, that the Madeirans heartily wished they had never heard of the word. 'We also have a local dance troupe who will come to perform, wearing traditional costume. Another inducement, perhaps.'

Oh, lord. 'What time does it begin?' she asked fatalistically.

'At eight o'clock.'

'Then I should be delighted,' she promised, and she did try to infuse some enthusiasm into her words, only she didn't think she succeeded very well. Checking her watch, to see it had just gone five, she added, 'I'll have a rest first, I think. Thank you for showing me round, and I promise to give your ideas some consideration. It's a pity it isn't nearer to the golf course; however, perhaps you could run a bus service, or something. I can't give any guarantees because I haven't yet seen the golf course, but I will give it some consideration.'

'Then that is all I ask, and I thank you for your kindness.' With a warm smile, and a rather touching little bow, he escorted her out to the lift.

It was so damned difficult to be offputting to people with such exquisite manners. From street sweeper to bank clerk, all were courteous, polite, and it made it very hard to deny them. Pushing into her room, the first thing she saw was the lavender track-suit folded neatly on the chair. For two pins she would have hurled it from the window, and it was only the fact that the maid had obviously taken the trouble to have it washed and pressed that prevented her. At least that was what she told herself, because she sure as hell didn't want, or need, any reminders of Kiel and the kindness he had once shown.

When she went down for her meal at seven, feeling slightly more refreshed after her sleep, she was thankful to find no sign of Kiel, although it was probably his malicious spirit that ensured remembrance. The meal was *espada* again. Swordfish. It even had another lousy fried banana lying on top.

Eventually abandoning any pretence at eating, she made her way to the disco room and was surprised to find it crowded. Perhaps she had better revise her thinking about the *fado* singer. Just because she hadn't heard of her didn't mean she wasn't good, or famous. Ordering herself a fruit juice, wishing that for once she could indulge in a vodka and get roaring drunk, she found a seat at the far side of the room. Everyone else seemed to be in groups and she was beginning to wish she hadn't come. The glances she received weren't only curious, but pitying as well, she decided crossly.

When the light dimmed, she roused herself sufficiently to look up, and her eyes clashed with Kiel's. He was lounging against a nearby wall, staring at her. So handsome, so impossibly handsome, she thought drearily. Dragging her eyes away, she fixed them determinedly on the floor where a young woman, dressed entirely in black, was standing, head bowed. There was no music, no guitar, as Justine had half expected, just the woman, and, whatever she had been expecting, it wasn't what she heard. Her voice sent a long shiver down Justine's spine, stood the hairs on the back of her neck on end, seemed to squeeze her insides. She didn't need to understand the words, know the language; the rough husky tones said it all. The pain, the loving, the dying, the emptiness, and she wanted to weep for all the pain and suffering in the world. Not for herself, the voice somehow made you see outside yourself, dismiss your own pain as trivial by comparison. The long high notes, the shuddering, almost guttural sounds that issued from that remarkable woman would stay with Justine as long as she lived. As the last quivering note died away, there was silence, as though everything had stopped, hearts, breath, living—and then the applause broke out. Thunderous, deafening. The room rose as one, and began to stamp and clap. Hidden by the people around her, Justine stayed in her seat, more emotionally aware than she had ever been in her life.

Wanting only to escape before she made a complete and utter fool of herself, she made her way to the exit. The applause was dying as people resumed their seats, exhausted by the emotion expended by that extraordinary woman. She didn't think the local dance troupe would have any success after that.

Her eyes blurred with tears, she made her way to the lift, then halted crossly when David called her. Swinging slowly round, sorely tempted not to talk to him, she gave in at his look of entreaty.

'I'm sorry, Jus,' he apologised quietly. 'I didn't mean not to be understanding. Ever since you left, I've been thinking about it. You were right, I am a selfish bastard, and, believe it or not, you are the last person I would want to hurt.'

'It doesn't matter,' she denied listlessly.

'Yes, it does.' Looking worried, he put a gentle hand on her shoulder. 'Are you all right? You look terrible.'

'Just a headache, David—I'll be fine. Goodnight.' Turning away, she turned reluctantly back when he caught her arm.

'I can't leave you like this,' he said unhappily. 'I never thought about, well, about how you would feel, I mean, about what you said. I was shocked, I suppose. Maybe if it had been anyone else but him . . .'

'It doesn't matter,' she denied tiredly. 'Go back to your Katia, and, if you've got any sense, be masterful. The Katias of this world like to be dominated. And if you hate the boat-yard so much, then get out. Do something you do want.'

'Like what? I can't and won't live on Katia's money!'

'I'm very glad to hear it,' she retorted impatiently. God, all she wanted was her bed, and all David wanted was for her to be his conscience. 'Why not go back to your painting? It was something you always loved, and were good at. It seems such a waste of talent.'

'But how?'

'I don't know, do I?' she exclaimed irritably. 'Paint people's yachts! There must be a market for that! Whenever I've ever been anywhere near sailing people, they always have pictures of yachts! Find the rich and famous—like, well, whoever,' she muttered. 'A lot of them must go sailing! Charge them the earth. You don't have to go back into the yard, it's not compulsory.'

'I know, but ever since the hotel idea folded . . .'

'Oh, for goodness' sake! Don't tell me you blame me for that as well! I told Katia, and her blasted brother, that it would never have worked!'

'I'm not blaming you! I know damned well it wouldn't have worked. I was only going to say that ever since that idea folded she's been restless, irritable.'

'Well, of course she has! I'm no authority on the subject, but I believe pregnant women often are! Anyway,' she added with a crotchety little twitch, 'I'm not a marriage counsellor; you'll have to sort out your own prob...' Suddenly registering his stunned expression, she let her breath out on a long sigh. 'Oh, hell. You didn't know, did you?'

Shaking his head, he just stared at her.

'Well, don't look so horrified! Don't you want a baby?'

'Yes. No. A baby?' he asked incredulously. 'Are you sure?'

'Well, so Kiel said...'

'A baby,' he repeated blankly. 'Why didn't she tell me?'

'I don't know, do I?' she demanded wearily.

'And I told her... Left her that note...'

Aching with tiredness, she patted his arm and turned away. 'I'm tired, David. Goodnight, I'll see you at the airport, I expect. Did you manage to get a seat?'

'What? Oh, yes. Justine?'

'Now what?' she demanded. Catching a movement from the corner of her eyes, she turned her head. Kiel was standing half hidden in the doorway beside them. Her mouth tight, she enunciated coldly, 'This is a private conversation!'

With a nasty little smile, he strolled past them to the lift. Turning back to David, her eyes bleak, she repeated irritably, 'What?'

'I was only going to ask,' he began hesitantly, 'if you knew where my car was...'

Staring at him in disbelief, she began to laugh. 'Oh, David,' she exclaimed helplessly.

'I know it's not the highest thing on your priority list,' he said sheepishly with a faint smile of his own, 'but I would like to know where it is.'

'I don't know where it is,' she confessed tiredly. 'You'll have to ask Kiel. He had it towed to a garage...'

'Towed?' he exclaimed in horror.

'Only because the wing was slightly buckled and dragging on the tyre,' she put in hastily. 'Anyway, I expect the police will give you the details if you ask. You'll need to see them anyway for the insurance. Or maybe Kiel has the details, I don't know. Now goodnight,' she said again with flat finality. Seeing the lift area free of Kiel's presence, she walked across and stabbed the button, then gave David an impatient glance when he shuffled up beside her.

'I'll tell him the truth, Jus, if it's important to you——'

'No!' she broke in. 'I don't want you to tell him anything!' And she didn't. If Kiel couldn't believe her explanation, then he wasn't likely to believe anyone else's. Certainly not David's. Anyway, she didn't care now whether he knew the truth or not. It was all immaterial. She'd never forgive him for his nastiness. Never. Even if he begged on bended knee!

When she finally reached her room, it was to find a note had been pushed under her door, together with her airline ticket. Tossing the ticket on to the dresser, she opened the note. 'The airport taxi has been ordered for nine o'clock,' she read. That was all. No signature, just the blunt facts. Ordered, which, translated, presumably meant she could either go with him or make her own arrangements. Tossing the note to join the ticket, she prepared for bed. Leaving out only what she would need for the morning, she packed her case. Going across to the window, she threw open the shutters that the maid always insisted on closing. When she leaned out she was surprised to find that it was raining. Not particularly hard, but raining nevertheless; then she wondered why she was surprised. Everyone had rain, didn't they? Even Madeira.

The gentle rain turned to a downpour during the night and Justine was forced to get up and close the shutters. Lightning forked the dark sky with jagged brilliance and thunder pounded between the peaks like some terrible symphony. She hadn't expected to get back to sleep with all that racket, but she must have drifted off because the next thing she knew was the little maid bringing her tea.

'*Bom dia,*' she mumbled. She felt a slight soreness in her throat, a muzziness in her head. No doubt due to all her grizzling.

'*Bom dia,*' the maid smiled. 'It is very wet. Very,' she emphasised. 'I hope your plane is not delayed.'

'Oh, hell, so do I,' Justine exclaimed. Scrambling out of bed, she hurried to the window and pushed the shutters wide. Wet? she thought in astonishment. Wet? It was a torrential downpour! And the road into town—well, wasn't! It was a river! Leaning further out, enabling her to see down into the town, she watched in astonishment as people continued about their normal business up to their knees in water. Their only concessions, as far as she could see, were umbrellas. 'Does it often get like this?' she asked faintly. Judging by the lack of surprise the maid was showing, it would certainly seem so.

'*Sim*, always water from mountains run into town. There are—*levada*?'

'*Levada?* Oh, drains? Gulleys?' she exclaimed as enlightenment dawned. They were all over the place, deep concrete gulleys that took the water from the mountains and channelled it safely away from crops and vines, and to stop topsoil being washed away. And if she'd thought about it she would have realised that when it rained, certainly as it was doing now, villages and towns were bound to get flooded, especially those that were low down, like Machico. Was the airport low down? She couldn't remember. Oh, God, please don't let the flight be delayed, she prayed. Being stuck with Kiel for a few more days would be unendurable.

Kiel had already checked them both out when she went down and both he and the manager were standing in the doorway looking out at the rain. A barricade had been built to stop the water flooding into the hotel, and as she joined them the manager smiled.

'The driver says he will try his best to get to the airport. The flights are leaving, but...' Shrugging, he indicated the state of the road. 'If you cannot get there, you must return. But in the hope that you may complete your journey, I would like to thank you for your kindness in allowing me to impose.'

'It was no imposition,' she denied with a faint smile, 'and as soon as I decide anything I will let you know. Hopefully I will be able to come again to see more of your beautiful island.' She knew she sounded stilted, unnatural, but was unable to help it with Kiel standing there listening to every word.

Escorting them over the barrier, the manager shook hands with them both before opening the rear door for Justine.

Kiel chose to sit in front with the driver. He neither looked at her nor acknowledged her presence, which suited her just fine. She wanted nothing whatever to do with him, and the sooner they parted company, the happier she would be. With a little wave to the manager as they set off, she settled back in her seat. The water in the bay, which had been so blue and sparkling the day before, was now a muddy brown with branches and debris being tossed helplessly in the surf.

As they ascended the steep hill, the driver for once showing caution, she looked back towards the town and gave a faint smile. All that could be seen of the people were the large black umbrellas. They looked like an army of water beetles performing a complicated dance. It would have been nice to have shared the sight with someone; to exclaim at the devastation, but there was no one, so she stayed silent.

With the engine labouring in low gear, they made their slow way towards the airport. It was only five miles, but at this rate it was going to take a long time and she began to worry that they might miss their flight. The further they got from the town, the worse the roads seemed to be, and if they had to get out and walk she was going to get soaked. Stupidly, she had packed her jacket and was wearing only a cotton shirt and jeans. Kiel had been more sensible; he was wearing his brown leather jacket. She was about to ask the driver to stop so that she could retrieve hers from her case when they screeched to a halt. Peering forward through the rain-lashed windscreen, she saw a mountain of mud and rubbish in front of them, completely blocking the road, and she didn't need the driver's curse, or Kiel's expletive, to tell her that this was as far as they were going. In the taxi, at any rate.

When the two men climbed out and began a huddled conversation, Justine too got out, and was soaked within seconds. Walking round to stand at the foot of the landslide, she kicked irritably at a loose boulder.

'Very helpful,' Kiel retorted scathingly.

Snapping round, she snarled, 'You cope your way, and I'll cope mine! If I want to kick boulders I'll damn well do so! And if I want to lie on the ground and scream, I'll do that too!' Swinging away from him, she marched defiantly up the mud pile, her temper giving her the balance and momentum she would otherwise have lacked. Staring out over the other side, her eyes narrowed against the rain, she saw the airport. About half a mile, she guessed, and although the road was blocked she could see it wouldn't be impossible to get down. Certainly the thought of spending another night anywhere near Kiel was an incentive to at least try.

Slipping and sliding back to the car, she collected her case. 'Have you settled up with the driver?' she asked haughtily.

'Yes,' he snapped with hostile precision.

'Good.' Turning away from him and putting her case at her feet, she reached into her pocket for the *escudos* she had changed and not used. Passing them across to the driver with a strained smile, she muttered, '*Obrigada. Muita obrigada*, thank you very much.' Still not looking at Kiel, she picked up her case and struggled back up the mound. With her case banging uncomfortably against her leg, her bag continually slipping off her shoulder, she struggled on. For some silly reason, she wanted to reach the airport before him and in her determined effort to outpace him she lost her balance and fell to her knees. Almost sobbing with frustration, she turned on Kiel like a wildcat when he attempted to help her to her feet.

'Don't touch me!' she yelled. 'I can manage by myself!'

Giving her a look of fury, he wrenched the suitcase out of her hand and stormed away. He seemed to easily keep his balance on the slippery ground and she glared after him, wishing she had the courage to throw a rock at him.

Wiping the wet hair off her face with a muddy hand, she struggled to her feet. By the time she reached the airport, she was exhausted. Soaking wet and covered in mud, she leaned tiredly against the glass wall to regain her breath. There was no sign of David or Kiel. She could have drowned out there for all they cared. Fallen and broken her leg. Any number of disasters could have befallen her, and would they have cared? No. They didn't even have the courtesy to wait and see if she arrived.

'The flight has been called,' Kiel said coldly from behind her.

Swinging round, she glared at him, not in the least grateful that he had in fact waited to make sure of her safety. 'Then we had better go, hadn't we?' she asked waspishly.

'As you say. I was unable to book your case in . . .'

'Why?' she demanded.

'Because the luggage has already been sent on board,' he informed her between his teeth. Turning on his heel, he walked off towards the departure lounge.

With a disdainful sniff, she followed him.

David had kept a seat free beside himself, and she gave him a glare as well when he exclaimed over her wet state. He, naturally, was bone dry.

'I rang Katia,' he told her with what she would have thought of as engaging boyishness had she been in a better mood.

'Did you? Good.'

'I explained everything.' With a little smile, that Justine thought extremely smug, he added softly, 'Funny to think of me as a dad.'

'Yeah. Hysterical.' His look of reproach made her feel like a worm, and as soon as they took off and the seatbelt sign was extinguished she hurried away to the tiny toilet cubicle and locked herself away. At least this way she could have a little cry in peace while she changed into dry clothes.

They landed at Heathrow to grey skies and a chilly wind and while David went to wait for his case to be unloaded she perched on a broken trolley. Kiel leaned against the wall nearby, a large, remote stranger. She didn't miss the looks thrown his way by other women, some of them quite blatant. Not that it seemed to be doing them any good; his face was as cold as charity, his green eyes arctic. When she spotted David threading his way towards them, she got wearily to her feet, only to be knocked flying by a middle-aged woman impatiently pushing through the throng.

Sounding for all the world as though he couldn't care less one way or the other as he helped her to her feet, Kiel asked flatly, 'Are you all right?'

'Yes,' she muttered. Shrugging away from his hold, she would have fallen if he hadn't grabbed her again.

'Oh, go and sit back down. It will be ages before we can get through Customs in this crush.'

Doing as she was bid, in truth more than glad to obey as a wave of dizziness assailed her, she leaned back and closed her eyes. She should have eaten on the plane, it had been plain foolishness not to, although her present feeling of illness probably stemmed from the beginnings of pneumonia, she decided masochistically. That would show them. She might even die!

'Ready?' Kiel asked wearily.

Opening her eyes, she levered herself to her feet. Feeling shivery and achy, she trailed miserably after the two men. When they finally reached the car, she leaned wearily against it.

Unlocking the car, Kiel practically pushed her into the passenger-seat, then gave David an impatient glance when he climbed into the back with the luggage.

The drive to her flat was completed in silence, and when they came to a halt she stumbled blindly out, fumbling for her keys. Opening the door, and leaving the men to do as they pleased, she made straight for the lounge and collapsed thankfully on to the sofa.

'Oh, come on, Justine, make an effort!' David demanded irritably. 'Where are they?'

'What?'

'The plans, dammit! Where did you put them?'

Reluctantly opening her eyes, she stared helplessly at him. 'I don't know,' she whispered. 'In my desk?'

With a tut of impatience, he went to look as Kiel came to perch beside her. 'Want anything? A cup of tea?' he asked stiffly.

Shaking her head, unable to even summon up any resentment at David's high-handed behaviour in going through her things without a care for their well-being, she listlessly watched him scattering papers and envelopes all over the floor, until with a curse he slammed the desk-top down again.

'They're not there! Where else would you put them?'

'I don't know. In the bedroom maybe. Bookshelf— I don't know. I don't remember,' she sighed. Her head felt as though it were about to explode and she rubbed her fingers tiredly across her forehead in an effort to minimise the pain. When Kiel got up to help in the search, she put her feet up and lay prone allowing both men's angry voices to wash over her. Kiel telling David to take more care; David telling Kiel to stop criticising, and, when they'd finished wrecking her tidy flat, they both returned to stand in front of her.

'Nothing!' David bit out disgustedly.

Reluctantly opening her eyes, she stared at him unseeingly as she tried to think where she might have put them. 'I don't even remember you coming here,' she exclaimed pathetically, 'let alone the plans.'

With a sound of fury in the back of his throat, he threw himself into the armchair. 'Terrific! I've got a baby to think of now! I need those plans!'

'All right, that's enough,' Kiel said authoritatively. Perching on the sofa arm, he instructed David quietly, 'Go through it step by step, from when you first arrived here last Sunday.'

'What good will that do?' he demanded petulantly.

'It might jog her memory. Do you have any better ideas?'

'No.' Taking a deep breath, he did as Kiel suggested. Starting with his arrival, he listed all that he could remember up until their meal.

'Then what? You didn't have to be at the airport until presumably an hour or so before the flight, say ten-thirty, so you'd leave here what? Nine-thirty?'

'About that,' he agreed sulkily.

'So what did you do for the rest of the afternoon and early evening?' Kiel demanded impatiently.

'We made grand passionate love!' David shouted resentfully. 'I took Justine to bed and——'

'And we watched an old film on TV,' Justine put in quietly. The sudden silence could have been cut with a knife. Levering herself slowly upright, she stared from one to the other. David was looking at her blankly; Kiel looked capable of murder.

'You've remembered,' Kiel said flatly.

'Yes,' she whispered hesitantly. She suddenly had a clear vision of herself and David sitting much as they were now. David sprawled in the armchair, herself curled up on the sofa.

'Well thank bloody goodness!' David exclaimed sarcastically. Sitting forward, he asked urgently, 'So where did you put the plans?'

Her eyes blank as she tried to capture another elusive memory, she didn't immediately answer. When she did, her voice was hesitant, 'We had cheese on toast for tea . . .'

'Never mind the blasted tea!' David roared. 'Where did you put the plans?'

With a little start, she focused on him, and slowly shook her head. 'I don't know—I don't!' she yelled.

'I don't remember!' Smashing her fist down to the sofa, she suddenly and unexpectedly burst into tears.

'Oh, hell,' David muttered.

Putting his arm round her in rough comfort, Kiel said mildly, 'David, go and get some fish and chips or something. We could all use something to eat.'

'Me? You're so keen on fish and chips, you go!'

'All right, I'll bloody go!'

'Good! And if you think I'm leaving you here to seduce her all over again, you need your head examined!'

'I've said I'll go! And I did not seduce her!' Kiel retorted coldly.

'Oh, no?' David sneered. 'What would you call it? Just out of hospital with a broken wrist and concussion, not knowing whether she was coming or going, what would you call it? Kind caring concern?'

'A damn sight more than you showed!' Kiel grated angrily as he got rather menacingly to his feet.

'I didn't damned well get her into my bed! And she's hardly your usual style, is she? She's no raving beauty. Just because you were bored...'

Terrified of the angry tension filling the room as both men faced each other, and terrified they would come to blows, Justine scrambled upright, yelling, 'Shut up, the pair of you! I'm not a puppet to be manipulated!' Swinging round on her cousin, she enunciated coldly, 'And, for your information, I seduced him!' In any other circumstances, the shock on his face would have been laughable.

'You did what?' David choked incredulously.

'Seduced him!' she repeated. 'As you so kindly pointed out, I'm no raving beauty, so girls like me have to take their opportunities when they arise, and you have to admit, Kiel is a rather magnificent animal. Now get out, both of you. I'm sick to death of being argued over as though I were a mouldy bone that neither wanted but were too bloody-minded to let the other have! And why you, David, are taking such an unwarranted interest in my affairs I haven't the least notion! The only interest you have ever shown in me in the past was when you wanted something!'

Her breath coming in angry gasps, she threw herself flat again, and all of them distinctly heard the crackle of paper from beneath the sofa cushion. A look of frozen surprise on her face, she carefully knelt up and felt beneath the cushion. Withdrawing a folded piece of paper, she stared at it blankly for a moment before passing it to Kiel.

'I'm sorry,' she whispered contritely. 'I truly didn't remember.'

'But you do now,' he said softly.

'Yes, I do now.' The memory of David giving her the plans in the car was crystal-clear. She remembered her impatience with him, her anger at his rash behaviour. Remembered getting out of the car, coming up to the flat and putting the plans under the cushion for safe keeping until she could return them to the yard.

Taking matters into his own hands, David wrenched the plans out of Kiel's hold. 'I'll take them down to the yard.'

With an exclamation of disgust, Kiel allowed his hand to fall limply to his side. 'Do as you like, only make sure they get them this time!'

'I will! Can I borrow your car?'

'No, you can't! Get a cab!'

'With what?'

'Oh, for goodness' sake!' Walking across to his jacket, Kiel removed his wallet. Taking a couple of twenty-pound notes out, he handed them to David. 'And I want the change.'

'You'll get it!' he said sulkily. 'Can I borrow your phone, Justine?'

Waving a limp hand towards the hall, she collapsed back on to the sofa. Neither of them spoke until they heard the front door close behind David.

'I'll tidy up,' Kiel said quietly. Getting to his feet, he bent to pick up the papers from the desk and replace them, then walked across to the bookshelves to do the same there.

Watching him, feeling limp and exhausted, wishing only that he would go, she asked listlessly, 'Why didn't you run him down?'

'Because I want to talk to you.'

'There's nothing left to say,' she denied tiredly. Leaning back, she began absently to pick a loose thread on the arm of the sofa. Her face set in lines of concentration, she jumped when he walked across and put a large hand over hers.

'There's a great deal to say,' he argued, 'but in view of the fact that you look as though you're knocking at death's door we'll leave any discussion until later. Do you need to pack anything else?'

Looking up at him in blank astonishment, she said, 'I beg your pardon?'

With a gesture of irritation, he explained as though to a child, 'You can't stay here alone.'

'Why not? I always stay here alone. It's my home.'

'I know it's your home!' he exclaimed wrathfully. 'But you're clearly unwell, so you are coming home with me. No arguments, no excuses! And why the hell did you tell David you seduced me?'

'Oh, I might have known you'd bring that up!'

'Then why say it?'

'Because I thought you were going to hit him!'

'I was. I wanted to smash his face out of all recognition. And that was the only reason?'

'Yes.'

'Not because you undervalue yourself?' he persisted.

'No,' she denied woodenly. 'I don't undervalue myself.' Or she hadn't, until she'd met him. And stupidly, despite their arguments, the insults they had hurled at each other, she still wanted him, wanted to get up, slide her arms round his waist, lay her head against his strong chest, not have to think. With a long, heartfelt sigh, she asked drearily, 'Can we now please change the subject?'

'Very well. We'll talk again when you're feeling better. Ready?'

'No. I——'

'Either willingly, or unwillingly, Justine,' he warned quietly.

'Oh, God.' Too tired to argue any more, she got reluctantly to her feet. As she followed him from the flat, the sarcastic words she had flung after him in Madeira came back into her mind. 'Whither thou goest.' Ruth had a hell of a lot to answer for, she thought despondently.

The journey to his home was completed in silence. Justine pretended to sleep, and Kiel determinedly concentrated on the road. When they pulled in through the double gates, she reluctantly opened her eyes. The front door was open, proving that his housekeeper had been on the watch, and a reluctant smile was dragged from her as Melly charged towards them. Dragging open Justine's door, she just stared at her for a moment.

'Oh, good grief! What have you done to her now?'

'I haven't done anything to her!' Kiel snapped crossly. 'I think she's got flu!'

Too tired to insist that she hadn't got anything of the sort, she allowed Melly to help her inside, and after that everything was a blur. She vaguely remembered being carried upstairs, but then nothing until she woke the following morning. Staring round her, she grimaced as she remembered her weak-willed behaviour of the night before. Why on earth had she let him insist on bringing her here? All it would do was lay her open to more heartache. Throwing back the covers, she climbed reluctantly from the warm bed and made her way to the bathroom.

'And just what do you think you're doing?' Melly demanded as she threw open the bedroom door.

Sorely tempted to ask what it looked like, she contented herself with a look that said it for her.

'Oh, we are getting better, aren't we?' Melly asked sarcastically. 'Do you need a hand?'

'No. Thank you,' she added belatedly. Continuing into the bathroom, she firmly closed the door.

When she came out, Melly was sitting on the edge of the bed. 'Feel better for your little burst of independence?' she asked with the same mild sarcasm. 'I thought you were supposed to have flu.'

'That was Kiel's diagnosis,' she said with an expressive grimace.

Nodding, the housekeeper levered her ample proportions upright. 'Well, you're no raving beauty, are you? But you've got spunk, I'll give you that. Feel up to something to eat?'

'Yes, please.' Certainly she felt hollow, which probably was caused by hunger, and when she'd eaten she'd probably feel fine, and then she could go home, couldn't she?

When Melly had gone, she continued to stare blankly at the wall. Feeling unutterably depressed, she decided to have a bath and wash her hair—or should she wait until after breakfast? Oh, Justine, just make up your mind and do it, will you? Blinking back a sudden rush of tears, she turned back towards the bathroom just as the door opened. Now what? Expecting Melly, she halted in surprise when Kiel's large frame entered.

'May I come in?' he asked with cool courtesy.

'You look as though you already are in,' she retorted waspishly.

With a sigh of exasperation, he closed the door behind him. Walking across to the bed, he perched on the edge. Regarding her silently for a moment, his eyes on her, he murmured almost thickly, 'Put your robe on.'

'What?'

'Your nightdress is see-through.'

With a mortified exclamation, she grabbed her robe and held it in front of her. 'Trust you to notice and tell me!'

'And if I hadn't,' he said wearily, 'I'd have been accused of being a voyeur. How are you feeling?'

'I'm perfectly all right,' she muttered rebelliously. 'I don't know why you had to drag me down here; there was absolutely nothing wrong with me that a good night's slee——'

'Justine!' he thundered in exasperation.

'Well . . .' she muttered with a little shrug. 'I wish you'd just get to the point. Why are you here?'

'To apologise,' he admitted shortly.

'Apologise?' she exclaimed in disbelief. 'You call this being apologetic?'

Staring at her, his face grim, he suddenly smiled, then gave a little snort of laughter. 'Oh, come and sit down. You're hovering over there like a frightened virgin.'

With a disdainful sniff, she walked across to the armchair. 'Apologise for what? David?'

'David?' he queried blankly. 'I haven't seen David. Nor Katia; they've gone to stay with my mother in Edinburgh.'

'Oh.' Then what had he come to apologise about? If he hadn't seen David, then he presumably hadn't come to beg forgiveness for misjudging her—and what the hell had happened to her promise to herself to have nothing further to do with him? She should tell him to get out; pack her things; ring for a cab.

'I came to apologise for my behaviour. For the way I treated you. The things you said, well, they were true, and I haven't been able to stop thinking about them. As you so rightly pointed out, even had I thought them, which I hadn't,' he added hastily, 'there was no need to say them.'

'So why did you?'

'I don't know,' he denied on a long sigh.

'Oh, well, that's helpful,' she retorted, borrowing some of Melly's sarcasm. 'Do you normally go around saying things without knowing why?' And why on earth couldn't she just accept his apology instead of insisting on this ridiculous post-mortem? Was she trying to put his back up again? With a long sigh of her own, she got up and went to stand at the window. 'Well, do you?' she persisted as she stared rather blindly out at the windswept garden.

'Yes,' he admitted with a rueful laugh. 'You make me so mad sometimes, I don't know what I'm saying half the time.' Getting to his feet, he walked to stand behind her. Easing the bundled-up dressing-gown away from her, he put it round her shoulders then helped her slide her good arm into the sleeve. 'When you first saw David in the bar, I was watching your face. You looked so delighted, so pleased, and I suppose it was a form of jealousy. I didn't want you to look at another man like that. Even if it was only your cousin.'

'But I was pleased to see him,' she said helplessly. 'I thought...' Breaking off, she turned to face him. Staring up into his still face, searching the deep green eyes, she added softly, 'I thought, now that we'd found him, we could spend the next day together.' By ourselves, she wanted to add. Just the two of us, only, because she wasn't quite sure what he was trying to say, she didn't say them.

It was silly how you pictured things in your head. She had imagined that when he'd seen David, and

David would naturally explain there was nothing between them, he would come to her. Had imagined conversations, conclusions... Only he hadn't seen David, and here they were, both skating round the subject like a couple of teenagers. And even if it was resolved, and they both bared their souls, what then? He hadn't said he wanted to see her again; why should he? Maybe he only wanted to clear the air, so that when they met again, as they assuredly would at some time or another, they would be able to meet without any ill feeling between them. 'And that's it?' she asked quietly.

'No.' With a rueful grimace, his eyes avoiding hers, he added, 'I was perhaps afraid of a commitment. It had all happened so fast. I'd wanted you, not because I thought you were easy, but because I liked you, found you attractive. Only then we met up with David, and the doubts began to creep in. Suppose you had been lying? And if you were, then I had been taken for a fool. If you weren't, then where did it all go from there? And I was suddenly afraid you would want, expect, commitment.'

'Oh, no,' she denied, 'I made it very clear I expected nothing. Nor did I. Do you think I really expected a man like you, wealthy, attractive, sophisticated, to look more than briefly at someone like me?' Ignoring his look of astonishment, she rushed on before her courage deserted her. 'For me it was special, a moment out of time, something I would remember as beautiful, perfect. So please, let us at least be honest. It wasn't my feelings you were worrying about, but your own.'

Clearly disliking the home truths she had hurled at him, he turned away. 'All right, it was my own,' he accepted harshly. 'And are you saying that you didn't have any feelings? That you didn't want, need, anything further from me?'

'No, I'm not saying that,' she denied irritably. 'I'm merely trying to clarify things! Just what is it you're trying to say, Kiel?'

Swinging back to face her, his mouth a tight line, he bit out, 'Sorry! That's what I was trying to say. Sorry! Against great odds, I was trying to issue an apology.'

'Well, fine. You've issued it. Grudging though it may be.' Feeling miserable and confused, she turned to stare back out of the window. *What the hell did you expect, Justine? A declaration?*

'It was not grudging!'

'Well, it certainly sounded it,' she muttered. 'The truth of the matter is, you'd made up your mind about me when we first met, and were more than happy to have it confirmed, it seems to me.'

'Don't be ridiculous! Admittedly, all I'd heard about you from Katia—and dismissed when I got to know you,' he added pointedly, 'seemed confirmed. No one likes to be taken for a fool—and weren't you just as guilty of the same thing? You made up your mind about me and were very quick to judge on a few ill-chosen words...'

'Ill-chosen?' she squeaked in disbelief as she swung back to face him. 'They were damned insulting!'

'I know they were insulting! I was in a temper! And if you hadn't insisted on ramming them down my throat I would have apologised then!'

'I didn't ram them down your throat! I asked you to be honest!'

'Honest? How the hell can anyone be honest when they're in a flaming temper? I don't coldly calculate every word I utter in case it should be misconstrued later! I'm not a blasted lawyer! And, despite your denigration to the contrary, I'm only human! That's half the trouble, I am only human, with all that implies. If you will persist in putting people on a pedestal so that they become terrified of making one slip, one mistake that you would leap on and demand a complete explanation from motive to repercussion, what the hell can you expect but lies? You want a damned machine that only acts and thinks as you assume it should. What do they call you at work? Penelope Perfect?'

'How dare you?' she spluttered furiously, but now that he was in full flow, and obviously determined to air all his grievances, he didn't give her a chance to finish—and how an apology could spark off all this she had no idea.

'You're a prig, Justine. You expect everyone to act as you dictate. I bet you hand out advice right, left and centre whether it's wanted or not; run people's lives on the lines you think proper—well, you want to be careful you don't fall off that narrow little path you've made for yourself. I bet if you'd had the chance you'd even have asked someone whether your sleeping with me was acceptable!' Giving a harsh laugh when she flushed dark red, because her outburst to David had come uncomfortably close to that description, he continued remorselessly, 'No wonder poor David got himself screwed up, what with you moralising on the one hand, and Katia weeping on the other. It's a wonder he didn't kick over the traces years ago! And how the hell he could say you don't give a man a hard time I don't know!' he added savagely. 'You do nothing but!' With a last scathing glance that gave her no chance to defend herself, he slammed out.

CHAPTER EIGHT

THE echo of the door crashing to gradually faded, leaving an empty silence which only seemed to emphasise Kiel's words.

'I don't moralise,' Justine muttered. Flinging herself across the bed, she stared up at the ceiling. 'I don't.' But did she? Her face stricken, she pondered the question. Was that how people saw her? As a moralising prig? Penelope Perfect? Hadn't she told her partner what to do in France? Hadn't she told David to take up painting? Even going so far as to tell him what? And, in the light of those taunts, didn't her behaviour with Katia become suspect? It was only her opinion that Katia couldn't have coped with the hotel—and what gave her the right to judge other people's capabilities?

Had she rammed Kiel's words down his throat? She couldn't for the life of her remember now. She remembered shouting, but the actual words escaped her. She lay for a long time, just thinking about Kiel's accusations, and the longer she thought, the more instances of her interference she came up with.

Why had no one said so before? Because she wouldn't have listened? As tears gathered in her lovely eyes and began to trickle down her face, she sniffed. Did she pigeonhole people? Make them fit preconceived moulds? And why? For what earthly reason?

'Well, that wasn't very clever, was it?' Melly demanded as she burst through the door.

Rolling quickly on to her face so that Melly wouldn't see her tears, she might just have well not bothered, because the housekeeper quickly saw through the defence.

'Crying won't do a bit of good,' she added bracingly. 'Here, eat your breakfast.'

Her voice muffled by the bedspread, she denied, 'I'm not hungry.'

'I don't care whether you're hungry or not! You'll still eat it! Now come on, stop being daft and sit up.'

With a sulky sniff, Justine did so. Accepting the tray across her knees, she avoided the housekeeper's bright glance. Not that it deprived Melly of speech. It didn't. Unfortunately.

Settling her bulk in the armchair, she continued sagaciously, 'Prodded his temper and found you had a tiger by the tail, didn't you? Well, I did warn you...'

'Yes, Melly, you did,' Justine put in shortly. Stabbing her fork into the bacon, she tore it ruthlessly into pieces. 'And if you're about to tell me how to mend matters, don't.'

'I wasn't going to,' she said smugly. 'Anyway, he'll be back when he's walked off his temper, all sorry for having hurt you.'

'I don't want him back,' she denied disagreeably, 'I hate him! And don't you ever knock?'

'That's a sock that won't wash; you don't hate him at all. It would be a great deal better if you did! Anyway, he doesn't mean half of what he says when he's in one of his tempers. Mind, you did provoke him,' she added fairly.

Staring at the housekeeper through a wild tangle of hair, she accused horrified, 'You were listening!'

'Well, of course I was. How else would I find things out?'

'Melly!' she exclaimed, shocked. 'How could you? And then to actually admit it!'

'Oh, pooh, why shouldn't I admit it? I'm not ashamed of it. I'll run you a nice hot bath, that will make you feel better.'

She didn't think anything would make her feel better. When Melly lumbered to her feet and went into the bathroom, Justine abandoned any pretence at eating and put the tray to one side.

'Went and fell in love with him, didn't you?' Melly shouted over the rush of water.

'No, I did not! And why don't you mind your own business?'

'Slept with him, though,' she continued with a wide grin.

'Oh, why not tell the whole world?' Justine yelled. 'I mean why not throw open the window and let everyone hear?' Climbing from the bed, she stalked across to the bathroom. Perching on the little stool, she glared crossly at the housekeeper.

'It's no good looking at me like that,' Melly laughed, 'or telling me to mind my own business. Kiel's tried it for years without success.'

'I wonder he puts up with you at all,' Justine derided, then yelped as her nightie was whipped over her head without a by your leave.

'Come on, into the bath with you,' Melly insisted.

Reluctantly obeying, knowing full well that any show of mutiny or outraged modesty would be ignored, she stepped cautiously into the hot bath.

'And you know why he puts up with me,' Melly continued affably. 'Help is hard to come by.'

Snorting rudely, Justine snatched the flannel out of Melly's hand. 'I can wash myself,' she insisted crossly. 'And I'd like to know why everyone assumes I need a blasted nanny!'

'Ho, ho, I can guess who that was.'

'Oh, shut up.' When her head was tipped ruth-lessly backwards and smothered in shampoo, she blew her breath out in exasperation. The whole scene was rather nastily reminiscent of another occasion, only Kiel had been a hell of a lot gentler than his wretched housekeeper.

Giving in to the inevitable, she allowed Melly to wash and rinse her hair—only she drew the line at being washed as well. Her vociferous insistence was met with a chuckle, but it was the housekeeper who decided when Justine had finished. Practically drag-ging her out, she wrapped her in a warm fluffy towel, then plonked another towel on her head. 'Go on, into the bedroom.'

'All right, there's no need to push!' Traipsing back to the bedroom, she sat before the dressing-table and sourly regarded her reflection. She looked like a sulky child. Pulling a face at herself, she sighed, then scowled when Melly came to stand behind her and began to rough-dry her hair. 'Ouch.'

'Stop moaning.' Tossing the towel to one side, she picked up the brush and began to untangle the long strands. 'Not like his usual women, are you?' she asked conversationally.

'How would I know? And I am not one of his women!' God, the woman was impossible. She just wanted to be left alone, go over all that Kiel had said, not discuss his love-life with this incorrigible woman.

'That Tracy now, the last one, a right little madam she was. Only she wasn't as clever as she thought she was. Kiel might want to throttle me himself, but he don't take kindly to people talking down to me. Snubbed me, she did.'

'How did she manage that?' Justine asked drily. If the late unlamented Tracy had managed that, she deserved a medal.

'There's no need to be saucy, my girl. If you want my help, you'd best speak nice.'

'I don't want your help,' she denied irritably, 'I hate him.'

'No, you don't. But you'll have to fight for him. You hurt his pride, you see, so, if you do want him, you'll have to swallow yours. Not that I'm saying he does want you, mind,' she warned, 'but he's a man worth fighting for, don't you think?'

'No,' she muttered unconvincingly.

With a little shake of her head, and a really rather compassionate smile, she patted Justine's shoulder. 'Come on, back to bed, I'll make you a nice cup of tea.'

'Melly?' she called softly as the housekeeper was about to go out. 'Have there been lots and lots of women?'

'Aye, a fair number,' she admitted gently, then added sagely, 'He's afraid to lose his freedom, you see.'

Leaning back, her damp hair spread on the pillow, she stared at the wall. So that was that. Had she really been expecting anything else? When she heard the muffled slam of the front door, she stiffened. She could hear voices, but not what was said, or who said it. When heavy footsteps began ascending the stairs, her eyes widened warily. Taking a deep breath, she held it as the door opened to reveal Kiel.

'I have to go back to Norway,' he announced baldly. Letting his own breath out wearily, he came further into the room and closed the door.

Despite the fact that she had been expecting it, his words still came as a shock, and she stared at him miserably, wanting him, wanting him to hold her, love her.

'Don't look like that,' he commanded quietly, 'as though I had beaten you.' Coming to perch on the bed beside her, he picked up her hand and held it loosely within his own grasp. Staring into wide violet eyes that showed all too clearly how much he had hurt her, he continued softly, 'We both need time. I don't know what the hell I feel for you, not right at this moment anyway. You infuriate me, excite me, make me feel more alive than I've felt in a long time. You make me feel stupid, boyish, irritable, and confused.' Putting out a gentle hand, he slid it beneath the long fall of shining hair. 'I want to know you when you're well, when you're not in pain, when your arm's better. I don't know if what I feel is a lasting emotion, and this last week has hardly been a fair test on either of us, has it?'

Her eyes filling with the all too ready tears, she shook her head. 'No,' she whispered.

'Ah, don't. Don't cry.' Pulling her into his arms, he rested his chin on her hair. 'When I come back, we'll start again, get to know each other properly.'

'Yes.' As brush-offs went, his had been incredibly gentle. But then he was probably an expert at extrication if Melly was right about all the women he had known. Holding him tight, for one long, poignant moment, knowing it would probably be the last time she would do so, she gently freed herself. With an endearing little sniff, she managed a watery smile. 'I'm OK. When do you go?'

'In a few minutes. I managed to get a seat on this evening's flight.'

Nodding, expecting nothing else, she said huskily, 'Take care, hm?'

'Yes, I'll take care. And you. Will you be all right on your own? You could stay here...'

'No, I'll go home.'

With a rueful smile, as though he had expected nothing else, he added, 'All right, Miss Independence, but get Melly to call you a cab, and don't go overdoing things.'

'No.'

Searching her eyes, then nodding as though satisfied, he bent to brush his mouth against hers. 'I'll call you.'

'Sure.'

As soon as the door had closed behind him, she leaned back and closed her eyes, but it didn't stop the tears that welled up unbidden and rolled silently down her face. She didn't honestly expect to hear from him again—and she didn't know if she could bear it. It seemed inconceivable that in one short week her feelings could become so intense; that he could fill her life and thoughts to the exclusion of all else. Yet he had.

The first week was bad. She returned to work and was persuaded to go home, and it was a measure of her distress that she obeyed. Peter, back from France, promised to look into the possibility of including Madeira in their brochure. He personally would go and view the golf course, meet the manager of the Dom Pedro Hotel, do anything else that needed to be done. He could cope. 'Go home, Justine.'

Too tired and dispirited to argue or insist she was well enough to resume her duties, she went home to brood.

The second and third weeks were worse. They seemed the longest and most miserable weeks of her

life. Quite convinced she would never hear from him
again, she returned to work, more in an effort to di-
vert her mind than because she was worried about
the business, which as it happened was running like
clockwork without her. That was depressing. Having reluctantly given authority to Peter, she was
slightly chagrined to discover that he wore the man-
tle as well as she, if not better. Which was probably
just as well, because, if it had been left to her, sheer
inattention would probably have bankrupted them.
And still he didn't ring.

There was some good news. David rang to say that
Naughton's had got the order for the new yacht. He
didn't mention Kiel. Neither did she.

At the beginning of the fourth week, when common sense was still battling with despair, a large
bunch of red roses arrived. There was no message,
just a card with a drawing of a Viking, and for the
first time in weeks a smile lightened the sadness in her
beautiful eyes. The following week, more roses, and
on the accompanying card, printed above the
Viking's horned helmet, were the words:
'Naughton's Yard'. Did that mean he had returned?
Or did it merely mean that the yard had started on
the new order? Or did it mean nothing at all? What
was it Melly had said? If you want him, you'll have
to fight. She did want him, but would fighting do any
good? And if she didn't respond to the flowers or the

cards, what then? Would he get in touch again? Or would he think she didn't care any more? He had said, all those weeks ago, 'I want to know you when you're well…when your arm's better.' Well, she had a hospital appointment at the end of that week to have the cast removed; that gave her a few days' grace. Why couldn't the wretched man have made it clear? Because he was still afraid of commitment? You're making assumptions, Justine, she told herself; the cards were probably only meant as a bit of fun.

All the rest of that week, her emotions fluctuated between hope and despondency, and, in the end, it was desperation that drove her.

Five weeks almost to the day since she had last seen him, Justine parked her car on the rutted track that led to Naughton's Yard. Five weeks. It sometimes seemed as if he'd been gone forever. Staring down at her white wrist, she flexed it experimentally. It felt funny with the cast removed, light, weak. Was she a fool to have come? And you won't find out sitting here, will you? she asked herself scornfully.

Carefully locking the car, she adjusted her cream skirt before slipping into her matching jacket, and, with the nerves in her stomach tying themselves into knots, she began walking towards the yard. Kiel was the first person she saw as she rounded the end shed, and she halted abruptly, almost shocked to find that he appeared larger than life, more magnificent than she remembered. How could someone like that possibly want her? she thought despairingly. Yet her eyes ran over him hungrily. Over the shock of fair hair, which still looked in need of cutting; the tanned naked torso; the long muscled legs that were revealed by the disreputable shorts he was wearing. The little lurch her heart gave told her, had she needed telling, that nothing had changed. She hadn't grown out of him, away from him. Her feelings hadn't altered at all, only intensified.

He was standing on the tow path, his elbows resting on the rail of a yacht as he spoke with a dark-haired woman. A very attractive young dark-haired woman, and she nearly turned tail there and then, yet if she did that she would maybe never know; might spend the rest of her life wondering—and then it was too late. The woman turned her head, smiled, said something to Kiel, who lazily turned his head. Even from this distance, Justine could see him stiffen, and, as he straightened, her heart sank. He didn't look exactly welcoming.

Her feet rooted to the path, she didn't see the curious glances from the men working in the shed, nor the smile on the face of the woman. She saw only Kiel, and as he walked towards her her eyes flew to his. They seemed more green than she remembered, and she suddenly found she hadn't a clue what to say. Neither, it seemed, did he, because he stood silently in front of her, and it wasn't until someone gave a loud wolf whistle that he seemed to snap out of his reverie.

With an annoyed frown, he said briskly, 'We'll go up to the house.'

Jamming his hands into his pockets, he strode off round the corner of the shed, and she stared miserably after him. She shouldn't have come. She'd obviously misunderstood. Her face reflecting her misery, she trailed after him. As she too rounded the end shed, strong arms encircled her, and she gave a squeal of alarm.

'I'm sorry,' he apologised thickly, but he didn't release her, just held her tighter and buried his face in her hair. 'I'm as nervous as hell.'

Pulling back a fraction so that she could see his face, she whispered perplexedly, 'You are?'

'Yes. I didn't think you'd come. I thought—oh, I don't know what I thought. This is the sixth week, the week the plaster was to come off—I wanted you to come to me.' His sentences jerky and unconnected, he continued hurriedly, 'I had some stupid idea that you would rush down here, throw yourself into my arms. Monday I paced the house and grounds, walked down to the road God knows how many times, watching for your car. Tuesday the

same. Wednesday Melly threw me out in exasperation. And today, today I decided you weren't coming. You didn't like my cards...'

'I adored your cards,' she whispered. Hope and
happiness transforming her face, she hugged him
hard. 'I was so frightened I was wrong, that I had
misunderstood—and I did come straight away, I only
had the plaster off this morning.'

With a strained smile, he murmured huskily, 'Fine
pair, aren't we? I——' Breaking off, he shouted, 'Go
away!'

Swinging round in alarm, Justine saw the dark-
haired woman peeping round the corner, a wide grin
on her face.

'Just testing,' she said cheekily. With a wink for
Justine, she disappeared.

'Natalie, John's wife,' he explained shortly. 'Oh,
come on, let's get out of here, it's like living in a
goldfish bowl.' With a hand in the middle of her
back, he propelled her along the track towards her
car. When they climbed in, Justine's hand was shaking so much that she found it difficult to fit the key
in the ignition.

'Kiel...'

'Don't,' he groaned. 'If I touch you now, I don't
think I'll be able to stop.'

Staring at him, feeling soft colour wash into her
face, she swallowed hard, then had to clear her throat

before she could trust herself to speak. 'But if you feel like that,' she asked in some bewilderment, 'why did you wait so long to get in touch?'

'Because I kept telling myself I didn't feel what I was feeling!' he exclaimed, and his voice sounded as rusty as her own. 'I didn't want to be involved with anyone! I liked my freedom—but I missed you,' he added simply. 'I think it was the longest month of my life. So I sent you the roses without saying anything, just that stupid card—and then I thought you'd think I'd run mad, so I finished up my business as quickly as I could and came to England. And being near you, I wanted you nearer still, so I sent some more roses . . .'

'But you didn't have the courage to come and see me yourself?' she guessed.

'No. I'd left it too long, you see. Hadn't rung as I'd promised—boy, this sounds so dumb!' he said despairingly.

No, she thought sadly, it sounds like a man struggling to free himself. Putting the car in gear, she drove carefully, feeling like a rank novice. Flicking him a glance, she found he was staring rigidly ahead.

When she drew up outside the house, Kiel jumped out of the car as though being forced to sit still had tested him to the limit. Following more slowly, she tried desperately to control feelings that seemed in imminent danger of rioting out of control.

Melly answered the door, and, after one quick look at Kiel, she turned to Justine. Giving her a droll glance, her mouth twitching, she said slowly, 'You came, then.'

'Yes,' Justine agreed inadequately.

'Oh, for God's sake!' Kiel snapped at the house-keeper. 'Take the afternoon off, go shopping or something!' Brushing past her, taking the stairs two at a time, he called over his shoulder, 'I'm going to have a shower.'

'Oh, my,' Melly said softly, 'we are in a state, aren't we?' With a rich chuckle, she pulled Justine inside. 'Well, go on, then,' she urged. 'Up you go.'

Feeling rushed and out of her depth, Justine climbed slowly after him. Cautiously pushing open his bedroom door, and hearing the shower running, she walked warily inside. It was a very masculine room, chocolate-brown carpet and curtains, cream and brown throwover on the bed, and the patches of wall between the old beams were painted cream. Prints depicting tall ships also decorated the walls, galleons, clippers, all except the print over the bed, she saw. Curious, she walked across to examine it more closely. It was of an elderly gentleman, in a ruff, and his painted eyes looked wise, kind. Kneel-ing on the edge of the bed, she rested her arms along the headboard and stared at him for long moments. 'I love him,' she whispered foolishly.

'Then why not tell him?' Kiel asked quietly from behind her.

Swinging round, she stared up into his taut face. The muscles in his jaw were rigid, his eyes almost feverishly bright. 'I love you,' she repeated simply. When he reached for her, she melted into his arms. Her heart jerking unevenly, her hands shaking, she untied the belt of his robe and slid her arms inside to his warm, damp flesh. Leaning forward, she touched her mouth to his strong throat.

'Oh, Justine.' Crushing her impossibly tight, his mouth sought hers with rough urgency.

Raising herself on tiptoe, her arms round his neck, she fitted her soft curves to his. Her breasts taut against his chest, she pushed her fingers roughly into his thick wet hair. Revelling in the strength of him, the warmth, she whispered his name against his mouth. Her heart thudding like a jack-hammer, she closed her eyes tight and gave herself up to the mindless kisses.

With a groan that shook his large frame, he quickly undressed her, then, picking her up, carried her to the bed. The feel of his hands shaping her, relearning her contours, was an exquisite torture. 'Love me,' she whispered as she guided him to her.

Breathless and shaking with need, she held him tight, rose with him, held for long, long moments, before they both crashed back to reality.

'Oh, Justine,' he sighed as his weight descended against her.

Pressing her mouth to his damp shoulder, she felt tears blur behind closed lids. 'Oh, Kiel, I've missed you so.'

Transferring his weight to his forearms, he looked down into her flushed face. Her hair was tangled on the pillow, and his eyes darkened to the deepest jade. 'I need you,' he said softly. 'I think I need you very badly.' With a long sigh, he disposed his length beside her and pulled her into his arms. With his mouth against her hair, he continued, 'That first week in Norway, everything I did, everywhere I went, your face was there before me, haunting me. Your wide violet eyes demanding something I wasn't sure I could give. How could I fall in love with a funny little face with impossible eyes? How could I not? But I would tell myself time and time again that it was impossible. I barely knew you. You weren't exceptionally beautiful, you were little and crotchety, funny and courageous, and I couldn't get you out of my mind. Couldn't sleep for thinking of you.' Moving so that he could see her face again, he demanded softly, 'What have you done to me? What magic did you weave to put me under your spell?'

Shaking her head, unable for the moment to speak for the tears blocking her throat, she smiled mistily, unable to quite believe the words that were pouring from him.

'In Madeira, when I was so awful to you, I was jealous. I'd never been jealous before, I didn't know how to handle it. Then when whoever it was whistled down at the yard I wanted to thump him. You were mine, I didn't want anyone else looking at you, admiring you. I've never been possessive in my life!' he exclaimed comically. 'And now look at me. An emotional and physical wreck!'

'Oh, not physical,' she denied softly. 'Most definitely not physical.'

His mouth hovering tantalisingly above hers, he demanded softly, 'Say it again.'

'That I love you?'

'Mm.'

With a wide smile, she obeyed. 'I love you, I want you, I need you. All right?'

'Very much all right.'

'So?' she teased.

With a rueful smile, which held more than a hint of embarrassment, he murmured throatily, 'I love you.' Looking away for a moment, he just as suddenly looked back. 'I've never said that before. For thirty-six years I've very carefully not said it—and now I want to shout it from the rooftops—and if you don't stop wriggling against me, I won't be answerable for the consequences.'

Holding his eyes, she gently rotated her hips, then grinned unrepentantly when he groaned.

'Oh, God. Wretched girl. Hang on a minute.' Getting lithely up, he walked across to the door. Listening for a moment, he deliberately turned the key. 'Just in case,' he grinned.

'A bit like locking the stable door, isn't it?'

Laughing, he dived boyishly on to the bed.

Scrambling to her knees, she turned him over on to his back. 'Not bad,' she said thoughtfully as hands and eyes made a thorough appraisal. Running her palm up his shin, across his knee, and along his thigh, she murmured, 'Nice legs.' With a teasing sideways look, she moved her hand further. 'Nice flat stomach, broad chest, stubborn chin. Exquisite nose—slightly arrogant, but exquisite none the less. And quite fantastic eyes. The hair's a bit unruly, but I guess I can learn to live with that.'

With a wicked grin, he captured her wandering hand and carried it to his mouth. 'I'm so glad.'

Her face sobering, she queried, 'You really want me? It seems so odd.'

'It does, doesn't it? Ouch! That hurt.'

'Serves you right.' Soothing the part she'd just slapped, she gave a happy sigh. 'Tell me how wonderful I am.'

With a choke of laughter, he pulled her down beside him. 'When we were in Madeira, when I woke you from sleep, remember? I had a very odd thought. I wondered, purely from a scientific viewpoint of course, if we had a child, what colour eyes would it have? Green or violet?'

'Probably mud-brown,' she said flippantly to hide the sudden lurch her heart gave. A child? Oh, lord, there was a very real possibility of that. Why on earth had she not given it a thought? 'Kiel?' she murmured hesitantly.

'Mm?'

'Do you like children?'

Snapping upright, dislodging Justine so that she toppled unceremoniously to the floor, he stared at her in shock. 'Oh, my God. Are we having one?'

'Not right at this minute, no!' she said in exasperation as she scrambled back on to the bed. 'I meant, well, I meant...'

'You meant that you aren't taking precautions,' he finished for her.

'Yes,' she admitted worriedly. 'I never gave it a thought.'

Scratching his head, he looked comically dismayed. 'Well, neither did I. Oh, well, it looks as though we're going to find out about eye-colour sooner than we expected.'

'You don't mind?'

'Hell, no. In for a penny, in for a pound. Not only leg-shackled, but hog-tied as well.' Turning his head to look at her, and seeing her troubled frown, he grinned and pulled her against him. 'Don't look so tragic, sweetheart, I'm sure I'll be a wonderful father.'

'That isn't what was bothering me.'

'What then? That you don't want to be a mother?'

'No-o.'

'Well, come on, don't be shy. Tell Daddy.'

She'd have liked nothing better than to 'tell Daddy' as he put it. The trouble was, she didn't quite know how to phrase it. He hadn't mentioned marriage, only that he loved her. The two didn't necessarily go together, or not nowadays they didn't, and if she was pregnant she wanted a husband, not a live-in lover. Only how to say so? With a long sigh, she tried being oblique. 'Kiel?'

'Mm,' he murmured humorously.

'Melly said there were lots of women.'

'Ah. Good old Melly. If there's a pot, you can bet your life she'll have her stick in it.' Settling her more comfortably against his shoulder, he began slowly, 'I don't know about lots. Quite a few, I suppose. But not one of them ever made me feel like this. Like a big lazy cat that got the cream. Not one ever captured my interest for more than a few hours, or days. Not one of them had the eyes of a witch—and not one of them ever crept into my heart and refused to be dislodged. They aren't important, Justine.'

'And there won't be any more?' she asked hesitantly. Needing his reassurance, she didn't think she could bear to share him, and she didn't honestly think she would have the strength of mind to leave him if he strayed. And that was something that surprised her enormously, and she began to understand now how women could stay with men who treated them abominably. If you loved with the intensity of her own feelings, there wasn't much of a choice.

'No, Justine, there won't be any more.'

'I don't think I could bear to lose you, not now.'

'I have absolutely no intention of getting lost,' he denied strongly. 'Believe it, Justine, unlikely as it seems—no, no, don't hit me again, I was only teasing—I love you. I want you as my wife, my mistress, my companion. Mother of my children. I want to settle down into cosy domesticity. What's so funny?' he queried in mock affront.

'The thought of you in a pinny. You really want to marry me?'

'Yes!'

'Good!' Propping her chin on his shoulder so that her eyes were close to his, she grinned. Being oblique was obviously the way to do it.

'I want you permanently in my life. In my home, my bed, morning, noon and night.'

'Are you sure you'll be up to it?' she teased.

Jack-knifing upwards, taking her completely by surprise, he turned her over and pinned her to the mattress. Staring down into her laughing face, he suddenly became serious. 'I do love you, Justine. More than I think you'll ever believe. I keep having this irrational fear that I don't deserve you. I have a terrible temper.'

'I know. I've sampled some of it, remember?' Making a fist, she punched him on the jaw. 'But as long as I know you love me, I can cope with that.' Straightening out her hand, she smoothed his unruly hair back from his forehead. 'Do you remember the first time we met?'

'Vividly,' he laughed.

'You frightened me half to death!' she complained.

'I know. You looked absolutely terrified.' A gleam of laughter in his eyes, he murmured modestly, 'I have that effect on women. And I think I had some sort of premonition then that you were going to be trouble...'

'But you didn't like me! Every time we met, all we did was argue.'

'Certainly added a bit of spice, didn't it?' he grinned. Smoothing her hair back from her face, he added gently, 'I didn't want to like you. You always made me feel vaguely guilty, did you know that? You have a disconcertingly direct gaze that seems to cut through sham, and, because it discomfited me, I think perhaps I was more than ready to believe the worst of you. And David didn't help—hey,' he suddenly exclaimed, 'did you know he's taken up painting again?' When she nodded, he suddenly laughed in genuine delight. 'I couldn't believe it. We had an advance order for the new yacht, and he actually, off his own bat, approached the purchaser and asked if he wanted to commission a painting of it. They negotiated a price, and David actually managed to get an advance!' With a wry shake of his head, he pulled her back into his arms. 'The prospect of becoming a father has certainly done wonders for him!'

'Mm,' she admitted ruefully. 'Another example of Penelope Perfect, I'm afraid. It was me who told him to go back to painting.' Tracing a gentle finger across his mouth, she asked softly, 'Are you sure you want to be married to someone so bossy?'

'Oh, yes,' he grinned, 'quite sure.'

Smoothing her hand across his warm shoulder, she murmured, 'I want to keep touching you. In fact I'm having the greatest difficulty in keeping my hands to myself,' she added wryly.

'Oh, good. You have two good arms now, no need for half-measures.' Gently encircling her wrist with his long fingers, he asked, 'How is it, by the way? What with one thing and another, I forgot to ask.'

Suddenly amused, she smiled. 'It's fine. Perfectly capable of dealing with you, and, hopefully, your needs.'

'Then prove it,' he suggested softly. 'We have an awful lot of time to make up.'

They were married three weeks later in the little church near Kiel's home. Standing in the porch, dressed in a cream silk dress and a silly, frivolous hat, Justine extended her left hand. Staring almost bemused at the new gold band, she smiled. Her hand and wrist still looked rather pale and thin, but time would soon alter that. So much had happened since the day at the boat-yard, and her mind was still whirling.

Kiel had taken her back to Norway with him for a week to finish the work he'd left when he'd returned to England to meet her. He'd shown her round his boyhood home where they would live part of each year; and, with an endearing mixture of pride and embarrassment, his favourite places. When they'd returned, they'd entered into a welter of preparations. They'd put her flat on the market, arranged to transfer her belongings to his home in Southampton, booked the church, flowers, caterers for the reception. Her partner Peter had been eager to buy her out of the agency, and Kiel's lawyers were handling the paperwork.

Kiel, for some odd chivalrous reason, had insisted they sleep in separate rooms until they were married, which to Justine seemed the height of absurdity. They had shared bed, bath, and everything else in Norway, and she had found the last two weeks frustrating to say the least. Turning to look at him as he chatted with John, who had acted as his best man, she ran her eyes lovingly over his tall, strong figure. He looked unusually smart. This was the first time she'd seen him in a suit and it made him seem something of a stranger, until he turned his head and the expression in his green eyes turned her insides to water.

'Don't,' she mouthed. Feeling absurdly shy, she looked away. Catching Melly's eye, she grinned. The housekeeper had found their behaviour a source of much amusement, and Melly, being Melly, did not keep her opinions to herself. Walking down the steps to join her, she gave her an impulsive hug. 'Are you off now?'

'Yes, I'll take David and Katia with me. You don't need to rush; it will take me a few minutes to get everything ready for you back at the house.'

When Katia and David joined her, she smiled at Kiel's sister. They had, thankfully, come to a new understanding. 'All right?' she asked her gently.

'Yes, all right,' she agreed. 'I feel very well.' Smoothing a hand over her rapidly expanding stomach, she turned to smile at her husband, and Justine was enormously relieved, and pleased, when he smiled back and gave her a hug. Turning back to her new sister-in-law, she said a little awkwardly, 'Kiel is very happy. I am glad. For you both.'

'Thank you.'

'We can be good friends again now, can't we?'

'Yes,' Justine agreed gently.

David, obviously deciding not to chance his arm, merely grinned at Justine and helped Katia into Melly's car.

Their departure seemed to act as a signal for everyone else, and within a few minutes she and Kiel were alone beside his Daimler.

'All right?' he asked softly.

'Mm, it doesn't seem real, does it?'

'It will.' Sliding his palm across her nape, he urged her gently towards him. 'Whose idea was it to have a reception?' he asked huskily. 'It seems forever since I made love to you.'

'You were the one who insisted on separate rooms.' Sliding her arms up round his neck, she pressed a soft, teasing kiss on his chin. 'And it's a moot point as to who wants who most. I'm shaking so much I won't be able to hold my champagne glass.'

'It's not the champagne glass I'm worried about,' he grinned. 'I daren't even kiss you. If I do, I won't be able to stop, and if we don't go now they'll be sending out a damned search party.' With a final hug, he helped her into the car.

Turning sideways in her seat, so that she could watch him, she slid her hand across his thigh, then grinned when he threw her a warning glance. 'Just testing,' she teased throatily.

Putting his own large palm over her hand, he drove them the short distance to the house one handed.

Keeping her eyes on his strong profile, the shaggy hair that, despite being professionally barbered, still looked like a mini-haystack, she giggled as she remembered their behaviour in Norway. They'd been hard put to it to keep their hands off each other. Wherever they went, whatever they did, they ended up in each other's arms. Recalling their behaviour in the little climbers' hut when they'd thought themselves alone, her slight frame shook with laughter.

'Share it,' he persuaded softly.

'I was remembering the climbers' hut...'

'Dreadful girl, you're leading me into terrible ways. That's one place I won't dare show my face again.'

'Well, how was I to know a party of German tourists were using it? It was you who said it was always deserted.'

'Which will certainly teach me to keep my mouth shut in future. And here we are. Home,' he added.

Switching off the engine, he turned to face her. 'Has a nice ring, doesn't it? Home?'

'Yes, especially being able to share it with the most special of men.'

With a warm smile, he leaned forward to kiss her. 'I love you.' Then, his smile widening, he placed his palm across her flat stomach. 'How's my son doing?'

Laughing delightedly, she shook her head at him. 'We don't know that there is one yet.'

'There is,' he said confidently. 'Or there will be soon. Come on, Mrs Lindstrom, let's get these shenanigans over with, then I can take you to bed.'

'That a promise?'

'It most certainly is.' Opening his door, and swinging his long legs out, he walked round to help her out. Lifting her up in his arms, he carried her towards the open front door. 'To the beginning of our future,' he whispered softly.

POSTCARDS FROM EUROPE

HARLEQUIN
PRESENTS®

Hi—

Have arrived safely in
Germany, but Diether
von Lössingen denies
that he's the baby's
father. Am determined
that he shoulder his
responsibilities!

Love, Sophie

P.S. Diether's shoulders
are certainly wide
enough.

**Fifty red-blooded, white-hot, true-blue hunks
from every State in the Union!**

Look for MEN MADE IN AMERICA! Written by some
of our most poplar authors, these stories feature fifty of
the strongest, sexiest men, each from a different state in
the union!

Two titles available every other month at your favorite
retail outlet.

In March, look for:

TANGLED LIES by Anne Stuart (Hawaii)
ROGUE'S VALLEY by Kathleen Creighton (Idaho)

In May, look for:

LOVE BY PROXY by Diana Palmer (Illinois)
POSSIBLES by Lass Small (Indiana)

You won't be able to resist MEN MADE IN AMERICA!

HARLEQUIN®

PRESENTS *Plus*

Meet Reece Falcon. He's the elusive businessman who shows Diana Lamb that a fine line separates love and hate. He's the man who destroyed her father's life!

And then there's Leith Carew. The handsome Australian forms an awkward alliance with Suzanne after a lost child and a chance meeting bring them together. Can they possibly discover a shining love in the heart of the outback?

Reece and Leith are just two of the sexy men you'll fall in love with each month in Harlequin Presents Plus.

Watch for
ELUSIVE OBSESSION by Carole Mortimer
Harlequin Presents Plus #1631

and

THE SHINING OF LOVE by Emma Darcy
Harlequin Presents Plus #1632

Harlequin Presents Plus
The best has just gotten better!

Available in March wherever Harlequin Books are sold.

My Valentine
1994

Celebrate the most romantic day of the year with
MY VALENTINE 1994
a collection of original stories, written by
four of Harlequin's most popular authors...

**MARGOT DALTON
MURIEL JENSEN
MARISA CARROLL
KAREN YOUNG**

*Available in February, wherever
Harlequin Books are sold.*

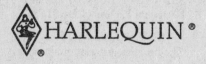

HARLEQUIN ®

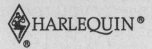

HARLEQUIN®

When the only time you have for yourself is...

STOLEN moments™

Spring into spring—by giving yourself a March Break! Take a few *stolen moments* and treat yourself to a Great Escape. Relax with one of our brand-new stories (or with all six!).

Each STOLEN MOMENTS title in our Great Escapes collection is a complete and never-before-published *short* novel. These contemporary romances are 96 pages long—the perfect length for the busy woman of the nineties!

Look for Great Escapes in our Stolen Moments display this March!

SIZZLE by Jennifer Crusie
ANNIVERSARY WALTZ
by Anne Marie Duquette
MAGGIE AND HER COLONEL
by Merline Lovelace
PRAIRIE SUMMER by Alina Roberts
THE SUGAR CUP by Annie Sims
LOVE ME NOT by Barbara Stewart

Wherever Harlequin and Silhouette books are sold.

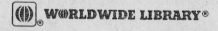
WORLDWIDE LIBRARY®

SMGE

Relive the romance...
Harlequin and Silhouette
are proud to present

A program of collections of three complete novels by the most requested
authors with the most requested themes. Be sure to look for one volume each
month with three complete novels by top name authors.

In January: **WESTERN LOVING**   Susan Fox
                                          JoAnn Ross
                                          Barbara Kaye

Loving a cowboy is easy—taming him isn't!

In February: **LOVER, COME BACK!**   Diana Palmer
                                          Lisa Jackson
                                          Patricia Gardner Evans

It was over so long ago—yet now they're calling, "Lover, Come Back!"

In March: **TEMPERATURE RISING**   JoAnn Ross
                                          Tess Gerritsen
                                          Jacqueline Diamond

Falling in love—just what the doctor ordered!

Available at your favorite retail outlet.

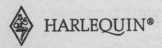

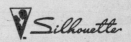

HARLEQUIN®

Don't miss these Harlequin favorites by some of our most distinguished authors!
And now, you can receive a discount by ordering two or more titles!

HT#25409	THE NIGHT IN SHINING ARMOR by JoAnn Ross	$2.99	☐
HT#25471	LOVESTORM by JoAnn Ross	$2.99	☐
HP#11463	THE WEDDING by Emma Darcy	$2.89	☐
HP#11592	THE LAST GRAND PASSION by Emma Darcy	$2.99	☐
HR#03188	DOUBLY DELICIOUS by Emma Goldrick	$2.89	☐
HR#03248	SAFE IN MY HEART by Leigh Michaels	$2.89	☐
HS#70464	CHILDREN OF THE HEART by Sally Garrett	$3.25	☐
HS#70524	STRING OF MIRACLES by Sally Garrett	$3.39	☐
HS#70500	THE SILENCE OF MIDNIGHT by Karen Young	$3.39	☐
HI#22178	SCHOOL FOR SPIES by Vickie York	$2.79	☐
HI#22212	DANGEROUS VINTAGE by Laura Pender	$2.89	☐
HI#22219	TORCH JOB by Patricia Rosemoor	$2.89	☐
HAR#16459	MACKENZIE'S BABY by Anne McAllister	$3.39	☐
HAR#16466	A COWBOY FOR CHRISTMAS by Anne McAllister	$3.39	☐
HAR#16462	THE PIRATE AND HIS LADY by Margaret St. George	$3.39	☐
HAR#16477	THE LAST REAL MAN by Rebecca Flanders	$3.39	☐
HH#28704	A CORNER OF HEAVEN by Theresa Michaels	$3.99	☐
HH#28707	LIGHT ON THE MOUNTAIN by Maura Seger	$3.99	☐

Harlequin Promotional Titles

#83247	YESTERDAY COMES TOMORROW by Rebecca Flanders	$4.99	☐
#83257	MY VALENTINE 1993	$4.99	☐
	(short-story collection featuring Anne Stuart, Judith Arnold, Anne McAllister, Linda Randall Wisdom)		

(limited quantities available on certain titles)

	AMOUNT	$
DEDUCT:	10% DISCOUNT FOR 2+ BOOKS	$
ADD:	POSTAGE & HANDLING	$
	($1.00 for one book, 50¢ for each additional)	
	APPLICABLE TAXES*	$ _____
	TOTAL PAYABLE	$ _____
	(check or money order—please do not send cash)	

To order, complete this form and send it, along with a check or money order for the total above, payable to Harlequin Books, to: **In the U.S.:** 3010 Walden Avenue, P.O. Box 9047, Buffalo, NY 14269-9047; **In Canada:** P.O. Box 613, Fort Erie, Ontario, L2A 5X3.

Name: _____

Address: _____ City: _____

State/Prov.: _____ Zip/Postal Code: _____

*New York residents remit applicable sales taxes.
Canadian residents remit applicable GST and provincial taxes.

HBACK-JM